Spinner of Yarns

RAY DACOLIAS

Spinner of Yarns

ISBN 978-0-9888177-9-1

Contents

The Lauren Tree

In the great human gallery of life, every person must assume an identity in society that will secure his survival. One person is called to be a farmer, another to be a soldier, some to mending wounds or being a merchant, a priest, a teacher or an officer of the law—and while a few wise ones find a position that defines them, most find a position that merely employs them. Rappal Musselweit decided early on in life that he would assume none of these or any other conventional roles.

"Human beings are loathsome pigs," Rappal said one day, sitting his child down upon the hard wooden chair in his house, "and are the weakest germ living on this planet—got that, boy?" and he slugged the arm of the child who dreamed of delicious cookies and bright red toys. "They can't believe that anybody who seems nice would lie to them; it's a wonderful weakness, Keerie, one which you can use daily to get great friends—all right?" and his face, the bright texture of the alcoholic who has outraged capillaries, burned crimson with rage. "Tell me what I just recently enunciated, or so help me I'll put the hand plow to your bare bottom."

Poor Keerie, nearly eleven years old, had grasped only a farthing of this rambling speech, and so his bottom received a potent beating.

"Keerie, you've got to listen, boy, it's for your own good," the terrible monster, as Keerie perceived him to be, began again. He had noticed that his father's demeanor would ignite into a conflagration at the smallest indiscretion Keerie made, and this left the boy on guard all day and night, and to quickly learn what the white-haired, flabby, pockmarked being desired of him.

"Hey," Rappal continued, a smile effacing the once searching scowl on his face as he playfully poked his son's belly, "remember when your dad helped you get new friends? Remember when Eddie was not being nice, and I told you to lie about Eddie, and soon no one liked him and then you had new friends? Remember how easy it was, Keerie? People are so gullible." He seemed to get angry at the thought of it. "Why are they like that, huh? I guess it's good; why do you think they are so gullible, boy?"

Keerie had rid himself of Eddie, but he had always felt unclean in the prosecution of the charade, and he could never again look directly into Eddie's face. "Yeah," he said, noticing that his father's tone demanded a positive reply, and Rappal understood this failing about him, and he frequently tested his boy for mental wanderings. This time, he used a tone that seemed to beg for a hearty vote of submission, when in actuality he demanded a screaming vote of dissension. "Well, what do you think—should we be nice to all of the kids, huh, yeah?"

"Yeah," Keerie answered, still daydreaming, and so he received a weighty slap across his dull visage.

It was the Monster again who stood before the bewildered child. "Now, you see that, Keerie? You don't listen, you just don't listen; now, why is that? You're daydreaming."

But I'm just a child, Keerie thought, unsure as to why this reason wasn't impetus enough to circumvent the beatings.

"You've got to listen, Keerie, if you want to get what you want from life; I mean, look at me, I'm an assistant manager at a big restaurant, lots of responsibilities…" It was more pointed verse designed to inflate Rappal's image, as all the while his black heart pumped his egregious doctrine of attrition and deception against his greatest enemy—mankind—through his corroded arteries and veins to feed his body with the wet pulp of animosity and contempt toward all things not Rappal.

Rappal, king of the kitchen, lord of the cash register, emperor of the employee room, plotted the downfall of those around him by using their humanness—their kindness, their charity—against them, a technique he had perfected since his first words were uttered toward his misbegotten mother. He would let loose a liar's silken web from his purple lips and smile as it attached its spindly form to its target, and then he would gleefully watch it move around its victim as it spun another strand and then another, and still once more and again and again until it was stronger now; and then the web would lift one strand, here, as it sensed another quarry, there, tightening another strand along the way to reinforce a previous deception, and then move on to produce another strand above and below and around to commence the entrapment of a new foe.

"Hey, Morley," Rappal said one day, pointing, and standing like a general in his green nylon top and black suede slacks, "that customer said you weren't very congenial to her." It was a lie. He wanted Morley to be more congenial, so he had invented a dissatisfied customer whom, he reasoned, Morley was too timid to approach.

"That's my mother," Morley replied.

Rappal's face never wasted a shade of worry. "No," he said, in disgust, "the woman behind her."

"I didn't serve her."

"No, no, not her," Rappal said, irritated, gesticulating about, "the lady with the hat on." There were three such ladies present.

"Oh," Morley said, resigned to defeat.

"Now, be more congenial so I don't have to tell Mr. Ajax about her." He did anyway.

Females were found to be the most naïve, Rappal knew, and were viable weapons to be used against the males.

And then there was Lauren, a girl with a merry sparkle in her emerald-green eyes. Her flaxen-colored hair sat in playful layers across her shoulders. Her beauteous face glowed with the charm and innocence of a blooming red rose. Her walk was light and graceful and strong, like a young, golden lioness who walks with pride amongst the fierce beasts of the jungle. She had no talent for hiding her emotions or inclinations, nor did she deceive anyone or seek their goods or positions, for their pain would have robbed her soul of its Virtue. When she spoke, her voice was light and wispy, full of an airy whisper and melodic song. Her tone was everything innocent and trusting, a living entity that expressed her gracious heart. "Oh, isn't it a precious day," she said this sunny morning, skipping into the employees' room, where her fellow cooks and waitresses released their stress and calmed their frustrations. "The sun is a warm, yellow ball of beauty today, umm," she said, humming, touching everyone on their heads and uttering blessings over them. O, how some of these young adults, vexed by their dashed hopes in a cruel world, ached to loathe her, to condemn her, to ignore her, but they could not; they wanted to curse her and revile her and make her cry just to make her miserable too, to make themselves more miserable, to hate themselves, to punish themselves, but, alas, they could not. She was the unspoiled, unassuming, loving creature they aspired to be but felt they could not be, for they felt the weight of the world crushing them every day and they could not resist its ominous touch; indeed, there was no world waiting for them to conquer except a world waiting to conquer them. She turned sour to sweet, night to day, darkness to light, and no amount of pessimism could dissuade her eternal optimism.

One was transported in her presence to the idyllic pasture where happiness roamed, so forceful was her magnetic aura of goodness. "Have a beautiful day," she sang, naming each of her fellow employees, and then she departed, injecting a spirit of hope into these drawn and tired youths as she sang a melody and danced all the way to her post.

"She likes girls, I hear," Rappal said to the employees immediately after she left, and this quickly opened a vicious perforation in Lauren's gentle armor.

It was as if he had detonated a bomb full of sewage in their midst, and now all of them felt unclean to listen and do nothing; they felt traitorous not to defend Lauren's honor and to allow Rappal to rip his bloody scythe down her soft heart and drain her radiance into the mire of slanderous gossip. "I know of at least one she's been with here," he breathed, another lie told to bolster the first one, to create suspicion and doubt in their minds. "Yeah, she's never with guys." No, Rappal, a perverse voice echoed in his soiled mind, you have wanted her from the beginning so you could control and consume her, but she did not want you; you have seen her with other men, but she was never with you; you have asked her out, but she refused you.

Lauren always spoke the truth; her words were always phrased not to offend, golden words always shaped to help the recipient, to inspire them, to bring them hope. Rappal, his words like daggers dug into their minds, continued on. "And she's always singing, too, like she's on drugs." They felt sick now, especially the young men, for it was as if he was laying his heavy black boot on Lauren's delicate white neck and grinding her into fodder. They knew, innately, that she was the finest hour of human being they had ever experienced, but they felt compelled to endure Rappal's malicious slashing of her sacred character.

Rappal's usual method of engagement was to seek out the victim he had maligned and tell them that it was a particular listener of Rappal's verbal slaying who had attacked them, thus planting doubt in their mind about their friends. Even though initially the victim might be incredulous about this accusation, sometimes they were ensnared by it; yet, this time it did not happen, for Lauren, responding to Rappal's deceit, merely told him that she never believed it when one person told her about another's words, saying, "I must hear them myself, of course; what kind of person would I be if I believed such anecdotal, scandalous lies?" and she trotted off, her face radiant as ever.

Those left in the employees' lounge were whispering frantically after this affair, for such events, though untoward, were tantalizing, and their mouths clamped shut when Rappal walked back in. He was smiling like a hyena with blood on his fat, greasy lips.

"So I says to Lauren, 'Lauren, would you go out with any of the guys here?' and she says, 'I didn't know we had any,' and finally she says, 'besides, I like girls better.'" Rappal stood like a father waiting for a confession from his children. A boy, not yet twenty, forgot where he was and who he was and agreed with Rappal's prior conviction of Lauren's character.

Two more youths fell into Rappal's sleazy chasm, adding spice and gunpowder to the blackening air.

An hour later, Rappal told Mr. Ajax about the appalling behavior of his employees toward Lauren. He told Lauren too, who again refused to believe such "trickle-down lies." Rappal could not confuse this fearless beauty, could not vex her, could not hurt her feelings; nor could he worry or scandalize her. These defeats cut a deep sore into his psyche, for he felt superior over all things and a burning desire to assert his will over them.

"She will bow," he vowed, incessantly; "she will be like me yet."

For three months, he picked off her friends with the cunning skill of a savage predator, though to her he evinced the face of the friend, the confidant, the wise counselor.

* * * * *

"People are so stupid," Rappal yelled, exasperated, yet pleased at his employees' imprudent behavior. "They believe anything, Keerie—boy, are you listening to me?"

Keerie was secretly celebrating the anniversary of a month-long friendship with his best pal, Hertzog, a friendship he had kept from his father, a man who had said many times that acquaintances too long become like parasites with beggars' faces, and that you should hold on only to people who can further your place in life. Rappal regularly interrogated Keerie's intermittent friends to see if there were any Rappal did not know about, and then he would give Keerie a deadline to not only dissolve these friendships, but to do it in a way that would gain him greater status in his school. "Yeah, sure," He finally said, refraining from calling him "Dad," a term that felt ugly and foreign to him now.

"Okay," he said, sternly, "what did I say—Keerie, look at me," and he clasped the trembling, small face of the child between his sausage-like fingers, "you want a whooping, boy?"

"Flattery," he said, instinctively, not knowing if he was right.

"Okay, that's better," he said, and he let loose and hugged him passionately. "I'm proud of you, Keerie." The boy smiled, and then Rappal slapped him violently across his white cheeks. "See what I did, boy? I used flattery to make you forget what I done to you; I know you guessed, boy; you got to stop day-dreaming all the time." He paused and then embraced him, this time for a longer period, massaging the boy's black, curly hair and scalp and narrow shoulders, and then whispered, "Sorry, Keerie, really," and Keerie sobbed and nodded, hugging his father. Rappal struck him again on his unsuspecting face, but this time the boy did not cry out, for shock had set in and lay like a wreck on his blanched face. "See what I did, boy? I set you up. People want to like everybody, and can't believe any-one would really use them, so when you say you're sorry to them, there's some weird thing inside them that forces them to forgive you and makes them want to like you, and makes them want you not to be sad or mean—to be like them. Can you believe that, Keerie? People are so stupid."

Keerie sat stone-faced, unmoving, his little body petri-fied by the height and depth and breadth of this latest brutal assault. Every day he was becoming more inured to the unso-licited attacks, yet he could feel something stirring inside he did understand.

His precious innocence was ebbing away, usurped by a sheath of rock ice.

* * * * *

Most employees of restaurants have the shelf life of fresh fruit.

These employees rot after the first heat wave, growing sprouts which feel their way toward other jobs that offer more dignity and opportunity. Because of this sad reality, certain hardy, mostly ambitious, sometimes scheming employees rise to the top in this moist, greasy environment, and they—without veteran employees to resist them—accumulate inordinate amounts of power; this was the reason Rappal could operate in this immature environ without boundaries, while feeding his prodigious ego on the noxious sweat of his trembling victims.

Lauren gave no concessions to Rappal, and thereby elevated herself above and beyond his station in life. He waxed angry because she would not submit to his every syllable and syllabus, and not bow to his every idea and affirm his every wish. She opposed him not directly but indirectly, opposing his illicit walkabouts on the periphery of orders and innuendo; she obeyed the seen, but not the unseen, and this gave him over to violent rants in his solitary moments.

"Let me be the tool to bring down the mighty," Lauren sang as she walked through the restaurant entrance on a Friday evening, dressed in the flames of love. "I am the minister of justice," she whispered, stopping still, listening to and feeling the bleak, rusty, shadowy air in the employee lounge. "Something once outlawed by God has awakened, its frozen soul turned to a foul liquid."

Rappal walked in fresh from a kill. "Hey, Lauren," he said, issuing the words through his clenched, yellow teeth, "you seem happy." He always spoke to everyone as if they were his friend, even if he had, only moments before, been forging their termination papers.

"I'm only happy—sayeth the philosopher—when I sleep, for only then I see no pain or suffering or injustice, and I can dream away the tyrants of this sinking Republic." She looked at him full in the face, her smooth countenance crisp and emboldened by fervent youth.

"Sure, me too," he said, ignoring the essence of her statement, and proceeded, as people often do, to another topic of lesser import. "Man, that Janus is so much trouble. Those Germans are so rude. We may have to fire him."

"So, you have intimate knowledge of the cultures and customs of Germany, I see," she said, cocking her head to one side, her blonde and arched brows knit in curiosity.

"No, but all the Germans I know are so belligerent and rude, so that must mean they are all that way."

"You know millions of Germans?" she asked, politely, innocently, smiling slightly.

"You don't have to know every German," he answered, exasperated, "to know they're just rude, greedy people."

"I thought you were part German."

For a moment, there was a quick conflagration bursting onto the weathered, ruddy landscape of Rappal's chewed, red face, but it was quickly recalled by its master. "Well, that's right, just a little bit," he said, and he held up his thumb and forefinger with a sliver of space in between, "but good German—and sometimes I am arrogant too, you know, but not like Janus."

"Janus is my friend."

"Well, he is my friend too, and I'm worried about him."

"You're going to fire him, though." Why, Lauren thought, he's backpedaling so fast he has to look behind himself.

"Oh, no, not now—probably not—oh, he knows, we talk all the time about his aggressive attitude with the customers."

"So, he's safe now."

"Oh, sure, yeah."

"Good," she said, smiling, that Lauren smile of congeniality that infuriated her enemies because they had decided it was a clever mask to cover her arrogance. They see menacing weeds all about them, Lauren had once thought of her critics, and I see delicate flowers.

Rappal was overtly friendly with Janus, but covertly treacherous, smiling and full of male bonding and good times, yet stalking and plotting and manipulating. When Rappal was with you, he confided in you, made you believe he was a brother, an equal, an ally against the common enemy—be it the management, the government, pestering girlfriends, or simply the injustices of the world. Ah, but though Rappal appeared to be a double agent, actually he was a triple agent, for not only did he betray his friends to these foes, he betrayed the foes to his friends—so in the end, he was an agent for himself.

"Janus, hey," Rappal cried, upon seeing the handsome youth who had hair the color of cinnamon, "now we can get some work done," and Rappal smiled, seemingly happy now. But one could never tell if he was truly happy to see those whom he disparaged, because sometimes he was truly happy to talk to his employees, and at other times he was feigning pleasure. "Have you heard about Mr. Ajax? He's really on Lauren for not being a team player."

"No," Janus said, believing it because it came from his friend, but not understanding the implication because Lauren was everyone's mother, nurturer and succorer of their pain.

"Sure, like the other day she squealed on you for taking a long break. Mr. Ajax didn't like that." Rappal had, in fact, been the squealer.

"No," Janus said, his thick, black brows knit, his skin becoming flushed with the tinge of outrage.

"Sure, and she's always in people's business, isn't she?"

"Well, I guess," he responded, disturbed. He was being ushered over the line of civility by the master, and he could not, in his brief youth, see the black web encircling his round head and pulling him away from the grounds of impartiality.

"She won't be here much longer."

"Really?"

"Too many complaints." There had been none, in fact, even when Rappal had tried to solicit ones from customers.

That day, Janus was quiet in his dealings with Lauren, and she sensed the treachery of Rappal coursing through Janus' thoughts.

A week later and Lauren was sitting in Mr. Ajax's small cubicle, being accused of coming up fifteen dollars short on her cash register.

"Only you and Mr. Musselweit had access to it on your shift," Mr. Ajax said, he of the short, squat form and bulbous, blue-veined nose. "This doesn't look good, Lauren; no, not at all, what with the complaints, too." And she heard the explicit details that had been drawn, by her tormentor, in a black, rich slander that told a tale of her false exterior and secret ambitions.

Lauren was unmoved, and her visage was calm and full of certitude, for she had understood long ago that it was wrong to attack your attackers when standing before the blind judge, and better to display humility and kindly sentiment, and in so doing reveal the true masquerader. She offered, therefore, no excuses—for what are they to a blind judge but an attempt to conceal blame? However, nor did she admit to any wrongdoing; instead, she gently nodded her head and responded with curiosity to the blunt charges.

Mr. Ajax had expected someone quite different from the sinister picture painted by Rappal, and not finding such an arrogant, contrary child, Mr. Ajax decided, in his growing wisdom, to let the whole matter go with simply an admonition to her. "Now, not another time, child," he said. "Fooled me once, shame on you; fooled me twice, shame on me."

"What about every day?" Lauren thought as she exited the little office. "O, Mr. Ajax, why do you always believe him? Is it because you need him so?"

In a month's time, Rappal had turned one fry cook, four hamburger-makers—was it that excessive protein in the meat these boys were devouring on the sly that compelled them to turn bad?—two waitresses—was it, for them, female jealousy because Lauren was what they were not, and knew they could never be?—and one hostess against Lauren; yet, none of the closing crew would follow Rappal's crumb trail to the gingerbread house, because they were a wild lot and revered Lauren but loathed Rappal, and these boys never believed his snakeskin lies, which always peeled off and created another lie that inevitably bit the believer.

Mr. Ajax, who favored the majority sentiment regardless of its philosophy, met with Lauren on a cold, wet, windy December evening to dismiss her from her duties. They sat in a dark cubicle, on old, creased black leather chairs, facing each other across a steel gray desk covered with managerial concerns. "So there you have it, child, you must be let go, eh? No way around it, so the statistics say," he said, his corpulent face affixed with a fatherly curiosity. "Why, not a tear or frown—do you hear me, child? I must force you out, the demerits point it out. And what will you do now, gone from us so suddenly?"

Her face was flushed with an intellectual kindness. "Mr. Ajax, it is my fortune that I am a member of a singular race that begs all people not to pay homage to misery over the humble self; so, do what you do as if it is righting a wrong, and pursue it with vigor, and think not of my fate."

Her smile bewildered the aged man, and his wrinkled face screwed up with a frown.

"Don't understand the whole thing myself," he said, shrugging his round shoulders; "why, you're the best employee I've got, loved by everyone—and by me, too, I am sure; why, I am sure of it; you're like my daughter! I've never had a harsh word with you, and you're always ready to pay another's debt; by golly, the whole affair is fantastic," he cried, smiting his thighs. His lusterless, weeping gray eyes narrowed, and he looked around as if to see a fiend lurking about. "Eerie," he whispered, leaning closer to her, "like something sinister is behind all of this."

Lauren, with her comforting countenance, created a smile in the delicate air that was part of a unique language, an elemental force eager to sink itself into all those immediately present. She leaned over and kissed the cold forehead of Mr. Ajax, placed a single red rose upon his desk, and said, her words dressed in tender love, "You'll always be my first boss," and she walked away, leaving a bewildered member of the bosses' elite corps to commence a radical act—to wit, to think of the actions of himself and others around him and analyze how they all interact socially.

Rappal had notified the other employees of the nefarious blossom Mr. Ajax had nurtured over the restaurant, and he proffered proof of it in the termination of the people's belle, Lauren. Thus established as the people's champion, Rappal staged an enthusiastic farewell to Lauren. He was first to applaud her as she walked into the employees' lounge, and then he spread that vacuous smile across his false face.

She saw the colorful decorations and gifts wrapped in glittering, gold paper, and saw her fellow employees crying, rushing to embrace her, this time to soothe her pain. It was the least they could do for their fallen heroine.

Lauren accepted every gift and farewell card as if it were handmade by her own family, and when the celebration was finished, and the employees were sent out to attend to the needs of the customers, she stood with Rappal, alone.

"Well, Lauren, I'm going to really miss you," he said, about to cry, and indeed he nearly was, for he had convinced himself that, for this brief intermission in his life, he really would miss her, but for reasons he had temporarily forgotten. She had been the ultimate adversary for him to conquer. Was that why he was so sad, he wondered?

She merely let her head cock to one side as she pronounced judgment upon him, her eyes gleaming like pools of liquid jade in a milky-white snow, "Beware all ye who injure God's children." She spoke it not with venom, but earnestly, and with conviction and humility, and then she departed, never to return.

One month later, Mr. Ajax was relieved of his duties by the District Supervisor, and Rappal Musselweit was elevated to the coveted status of Manager.

* * * * *

There is order in Nature if Man does not steal the Light that seals the Darkness, the Light that creates equilibrium, the Light that brings balance and harmony; but wound the Light and there will be a cataclysmic shift to compensate for the Sin, and then Nature, in Her vengeance, will be a Divine Huntress.

"Where is Lauren these days?" Rappal said one night, grinning the grin of domination unchecked. It had been forty days since Lauren's departure.

"Bringing joy, I'm sure," one of the young girls said, thoughtfully, and all of the employees in the room speculated upon the wealth of happiness Lauren had shed.

Janus walked in ashen-faced, his frozen face devoid of life as he handed the newspaper to Rappal, who quickly saw the article that had given no little violence to the youth's heart.

"There was a holdup attempt at the Doll's House Restaurant last night," Rappal began to read, with sympathy, for he remembered how others exuded shock and sorrow at such events. "Three armed men came in and demanded money from a male employee, and began to beat him when he gave them too little cash. The three robbers threatened to shoot customers if the Manager did not give them the money; however, the Manager was at the bank making a deposit, and this was an ill omen for the innocent hostages in the restaurant. Then, a female employee, a hostess, stepped in. Her name was Lauren."

"Lauren," all of the employees around Rappal responded, as if in a deep trance.

"Lauren," one of the young men shouted, about to weep.

Even Rappal gave the poor youth the look of the others, the look of doom, and the boy shrank back and collapsed in a heap of shuddering cries.

"Lauren convinced the men that no money was on the premises," Rappal continued reading, "and after one of the robbers shot a customer, she offered herself as hostage."

"She should be here with us now," a hard whisper began, dripping slowly from the acrid air.

Rappal continued, "The three robbers took Lauren to a nearby field."

"She should still be alive," a metallic, loud voice boomed in their burning ears.

Rappal read the nefarious affair of the three robbers, with a kind of queer eagerness that was still properly strained with sadness. The sordid details of the assault upon Lauren were beyond the imagination of civilized people.

Who could stand now? Who could think now? Who could smile, now, upon hearing of the unnatural impulses of these debased creatures that were satisfied upon a sublime child of God?

"Dead," the sanguinary song banged in the employees' brains, "dead because of Rappal."

Rappal was the leader upon whom all eyes turned for solace, and he gave them the sad, drooping eyes and the look of helplessness that he had seen other people evince after such a tragedy. He enjoyed hugging the pretty girls as they cried, and he thought of those fleshly delights he might later gain from this moment. "Now they will need me to comfort them," he thought, greedily.

Two days passed.

The first time he dated Sheila, Monica saw them together, yet Rappal managed to convince Monica that he and Sheila were providing emotional comfort to each other because of the tragedy of Lauren. The next night he was with Monica, and Susan saw them and he too convinced her that the dinner was to comfort Monica. He dated Susan the next night.

His power over human beings, his ability to manipulate people, to find their foibles and exploit them, grew exponentially. The Supervisor in the District Office looked with favor upon Rappal, recognizing him as their own kind, one they mustn't lose to a competitor.

Under Rappal's rule, he baked the sentiment of sorrow over Lauren's loss into a thick, crumbly, delicious chunk of hot honey roll, and he fed everyone this delectable meal until they were satiated.

It was a Friday evening, after closing, and Rappal was there at the restaurant, as he always was, for here was home and entertainment. He stood before the male employees, his sharp tongue and frank talk sloughing off the shreds of skin that unraveled from the sordid tales of his dates with the female employees. The young men reasoned they were in the presence of a romantic hero; had he not managed to puncture the carefully woven armor that all women spin around themselves until the right suitor comes along? And had he not managed to convince these women, against their natural instincts, that his intentions were honorable? He must be a creature, the males decided, born with the rarest of sweat pheromones that lured all women to him despite his meager appearance and mediocre station in life. They sat at his feet, pious and timid, as if he were a master lover.

"And then, you see," the guru of love further explained that night, "I went out with Margie on Saturday."

Omar, breathing in every word of his master, shyly raised his hand. "But, Rappal, you went out with Margie on Friday."

"No, I didn't, because I went out with Rojale on Friday."

"No, Rojale was on Sunday," Roman interjected.

The Master's oxygen-starved blood vessels on his ruddy face became even more strangulated as his swollen cheeks puffed out. "Hey," he cried, "I should know who I went out with and when," and then let out a long "geez," his favorite expression when he was exasperated, and one where he always extended the final sound for emphasis; and then he produced a nervous, artificial smile.

Yes, but he was, the truth be told, wrong.

"I mean, after all, they're all the same, right? They're just harlots thinking they can sleep with the boss for favors." His rage, like a living thing, invaded the heavy air.

But this wasn't what the young men wanted to hear in their anguished souls at all; they yearned to hear the secrets of these esoteric beauties unfurl like an ancient manuscript found, revealing the inner workings of a universe hitherto unknown to their immature minds. And now Rappal had spilled mud on their thrilling anticipation, a stinking, rancid spew of black mud that dried quickly and would stick on their faces until a good deed melted it away. One of the young men felt as if he had to go right then and there and join the Peace Corps to atone for hearing such malevolent insults.

However, Rappal, like any good general and strategist, improvised in the field. "I didn't mean harlots like bad—I mean all women are harlots—my mother is a harlot, if you look at the definition the way I do—sleeping with a man even if you're married to him, even if you love him, you're a harlot—heck, I'm a harlot, too—we're all harlots, really." His fat, hairy fingers were strumming the air, his purple countenance shifting like dark shadows in a windy forest. "Not a harlot in a bad way, of course, but harlot like getting something you want maybe not by laying with somebody but by a smile—that's a harlot, really, doing things for profit, I guess, or maybe just getting your way, like pretending to be somebody's friend, is a harlot. So, it's not really a bad term, the way I use it. Anyway."

He simply could have denied it, Omar thought, bewildered.

"They're all good pals, not harlots at all, no way," Rappal continued, and he smiled a smile that said it was all right even though the boys had an uncomfortable, creepy feeling in their lazy gut while cold sweat was trickling down their tingling spine. "I mean, look at Lauren."

At that precise moment in all their history, it did not matter if he was their boss or father or brother or college administrator; at this moment in their mania, they would have risked it all to keep the idea that their one pure, golden image in all the world, Lauren, would forever be sealed in their passionate hearts. They looked at him like hungry young wolves, who, at a fresh kill, suddenly look at their master as their next victim. Rappal's face dropped all known color and transformed into a lump of frozen fright.

"I mean," Rappal stuttered, halted, then rejoined efforts to communicate falsely to them, "Lauren was gold—golden, she was golden, not like them other girls," and he saw their tight jaws slacken, encouraging his further shoveling away of his intended injustice. "Even though those girls are all right, Lauren was really special," he continued, and he saw their enamored faces, and his face grew enamored too. "Lauren made every day special," and he actually became animated in remembering something that never happened, but he made it happen in his mind so he could produce it so eloquently to his audience.

A wise man once wrote, "The truth brings eloquence because there is no artifice to stumble over, and to believe anything to be true and speak it with pathos is the art of the politician."

And even though Rappal rambled on about more of his amorous outings, converging on spurious anecdotes and diverging on gasping truths, there was an air of weirdness about his heated visage, for he had continued to mistakenly identify the girls on their respective date nights. This was a breach in his cunning cloak of disinformation he now wore like an inglorious, thorny wreath.

The next morning, the same crew reported to open the restaurant, a schedule Rappal delighted in to foster loyalty solely to him, thus opening up a chance for them to rise up the Musselweit ladder, whereas disloyalty to him from them or anyone else would result in being hung on the bottommost rung.

Roman, upon seeing Rappal—who was his masculine role model—greeted him with a young man's hormone-juiced salute regarding the girls. Rappal looked at him askance, and then pulled him, with no little force, into the drink station. "Who told you about the girls?" he demanded.

"Why, you, Rappal," Roman said, still smiling, thinking this was a game.

"I didn't talk about nothing," Rappal spat, his bubbles of spittle floating down like an army of parachutists onto Roman's chin, and then he disappeared around the corner.

The next day, Roman was blackening his sweaty hands on the classified ads of the local newspaper, noticeably in the "Cook Wanted" section. The youth was slowly learning about the personalities who inhabit positions of power in the business world.

* * * * *

Flux was the action Rappal saw no matter the size of the situation nor its reason for existence; turbulence was Rappal's leather saddle in the midst of every moment of opportunity, and where there was human charity or compassion or injustice involved, he rode in on its saddle like a nuclear bandit to create chaos.

Keerie sat in a bloated daze, facing his mentor. Rappal, now emboldened by his unlimited successes, expounded on the virtues of treachery and deceit.

"If you're going to be a liar, you've got to be consistent," Rappal began, gorging on the thick meats he had gleaned from work. "Your mother lied and got caught lying because she wasn't a successful liar; now, I would have been more tolerant if she had the smarts," and he pointed, with the chunk of tender meat on his fork, to his head, "up here, but she wasn't. She would lie once and lie again, forgetting what the first lie was and then lying again about the same thing until she forgot everything—stupid." And he rammed the juicy beef into his gaping mouth. "You see, Keerie," and he said his son's name slowly, deliberately, "if you tell the truth and stick with it, you don't get caught in a lie; but to lie successfully, you have to remember the lie, rehearse the lie, live the lie and make yourself believe it really happened, and then you can't get caught. See?"

The boy still had not mastered this question-and-answer session, and he sometimes asked questions that did not further the discussion, but only succeeded in distracting from the topic, which was a major violation of Rappal's dinner etiquette. "I thought," he said, abruptly, forgetting all the previous meetings when corrective answers from Rappal yielded him only physical pain, "you lied to get rid of Mother."

There was a wet piece of partially digested meat flying through the air in the small space between Rappal and Keerie, a projectile spewed from Rappal's mouth, which landed beneath Keerie's right cheek. "Now," Rappal screamed, "we don't waste food around here! I went to a lot of trouble to steal that from those penny pinchers at work—so eat it, you ingrate!" Keerie obediently scooped up the chewed morsel and swallowed it.

"That's better. You gotta stop lying about lying—to me, but to your so-called friends, Keerie—to them," and he gesticulated to the outside world, "you keep telling truthful lies."

"You were the liar," Keerie silently remonstrated, "you've told me so many times over and over how you lied to get rid of my mother."

"Your mother was a lying harlot, don't forget that—a lying harlot."

"But you were the liar because you lied to catch her telling the truth."

Rappal's face sprouted tiny, outraged capillaries that festered like a field of overripe red beans. "You will not contradict your beloved father, boy," he raged, rainbows of puffy billows of spittle landing like assault teams on the steaming food. "You're getting like that idiot Jay, who got Roman fired."

"Why, you got him fired," Keerie responded. He never did understand why he was unable to compete with the impulse to impart truth into the wicked face of falsehood, and now that he had prevailed, he found out why. This unexpected outburst earned him a cool cup of raw, whole milk splashed onto his white t-shirt. The dinner rule in this house was that once Keerie was dressed in his father's meal, he could not leave the table until he had finished the food that was splattered everywhere.

"For lying, Keerie," Rappal said, watching his son stuff himself with the mounds of food his father did not eat, "you made me lose my appetite, and you know I don't put up with waste in this house; you know how that upsets me when people waste food, especially when there are starving little boys and girls around the world."

Keerie had never seen these starving people, but he had learned to loathe them long ago. "And why do I have to suffer because they suffer?" he thought as he stuffed down another chunk of cold potato. He felt his queasy stomach signal once more for termination of these proceedings by producing more ache, more nausea, a little regurgitation here, a hint of total rejection there.

At the breakfast table the next morning, Keerie sat, with ashen face and slumping countenance, having spent the better part of the night returning, vomit by vomit, the coerced meal and bitter gastric juices up his inflamed esophagus and out his gaping, spastic mouth.

"Come on, Keerie, you've got to eat, boy," Rappal sang, "after all that eating I did last night because you wouldn't eat your food, you should be starved."

Disbelief spanked Keerie in his delicate gut, and for a moment he actually pondered the benefits of agreeing with such a poisonous lie, but his newly acquired affinity for trampling falsehoods stiffened his resolve to expound the truth. "But I ate your meal," he said, without addressing him as "Father," a term he considered too respectful and too close to affection.

That morning, at five-thirty in the a.m., Keerie ate three bowlfuls of oatmeal, three cups of full-fat milk, five greasy clumps of cinnamon bear claws, and two cups of sugar-spiked coffee. This was his punishment for more alleged lies.

"You've got to quit lying to me, boy—save it for the outsiders," Rappal had said, disgusted.

That day Keerie ran away, never to return. It really didn't matter, though, because by that night, Rappal was going to be transferred to that bleak land where the exiled, naked tyrants go to dwell.

* * * * *

Rappal was at work that day by five-thirty in the a.m., inspecting the previous night's work and looking for imperfections in the work of his closing crew. When the first employee entered at six-thirty that morning, Rappal felt as if this person was merely a guest in his dwelling, for the yellow, glossy walls of the restaurant had become more familiar to him than his own.

This was to be a day of atonement, a day when Rappal would gain absolute fear and loyalty in his employees, a day to secure his position as golden boy amongst Managers. This day he would cut expenditures and increase productivity and profits.

He stood before the entire staff at seven o'clock in the a.m., the architect of a burning house into which he would fling some of their squirming bodies. He would be the author of their excursion into an economic funeral procession. He lathered the list of those executed with a teasing exhaust from his gaping mouth that leaked its noxious vapors into their tense nostrils. The Good amongst them knew their moment was near, those few who had not played his twisted game, those who had not persecuted their fellow employee nor falsified documents against their fellow man. They, the Good and Noble, understood the price for being recognized as messengers of God, and they bore their crown of thorns like martyred saints.

He, Rappal Musselweit, read the names of those terminated with a slow, melodramatic, revengeful slur, scorched by a terror-filled, intermittent pause that seemed to last a lifetime. Yet, after the first three names were read, an arc of revelation dawned upon the Good. "It is not I, nor my companions—nay, none of my own kind!" they cried in their happy thoughts. Indeed, Rappal had smothered to an economic death his own kind. He had unwittingly amputated the tics from their host. O, how the villains cried foul when Rappal herded them out with their check in hand; O, how they vowed to destroy him for his treachery; but the wicked had been wickedly handled, and Nature had leveled a rising rank of alien predators to protect its indigenous populations.

Rappal, gleeful as a newly ordained king, danced around the brown dining tables, laughing in a giddy screech which denoted the excess of power that he felt surging throughout his sinister brain. "Real stupid," he shouted, looking at the shocked faces of those who remained, "now we are going to really terrorize!" He extrapolated upon his daring plan that would take himself and these seven employees he supposed to be his co-conspirators to levels of hitherto unknown wealth and power. He enumerated the categories: falsification of gross sales, fantastic raises, promotion to the highest ranks for his co-conspirators, and all the food one could pack into one's truck. He boasted of all these things. He was going to follow this plan, yes, but all the while he would be setting them up for the fall, and then he would take credit for exposing such corruption; he would either use their rotting reputations to build upon his own rising star, and ditch them, or use their loyalty to gain a solid foundation, and then forsake them. He truly had not decided which.

Omar felt as if the gray eyes of Rappal proceeded into his own brain and found dissension. "What if," he wondered, aghast, "those ghoulish eyes catch the sound of my thumping heart that proclaims betrayal!" It was betrayal in the form of a miniature tape recorder in Omar's pocket, and he was afraid to even produce bad thoughts against Rappal for fear that his own brain would create a negative body posture or faint reflection of disdain that he could not suppress. Consequently, Omar thought good thoughts about Rappal and diabolical thoughts against the meek, all to envision Omar's happy, consensual collusion with Rappal.

That night, the seven employees met at Omar's house and listened to the contents of the tape. "It's as if," Omar said, grim faced, "we have intercepted a master plan to exterminate an entire Race."

Friday came and the District Manager, after hearing the tape and seeing the evidence provided by the seven employees, terminated Rappal from his managerial position.

Five days later, the District Manager terminated the seven employees from their menial positions.

Sayeth the philosopher, "Power is like a virulent virus in the intestines of society—once infested, the virus is willing to abrogate all threats or perceived threats to itself."

* * * * *

Rappal's mind had hatched a poisoned egg that gave birth to skewed visions where all previous concepts and laws and correspondence with the world were tossed into a molten sea of insanity; in his black soul sprung a new order with a biography of the world created by his own squirming mind. The process that had begun not too long ago had now been completed.

"Well, Rappal, you did good, boy, real good," Rappal said to himself a week later, admiring his naked form in the mirror. "Getting fired was real smart, boy, real good." He slapped his soft, white belly. "I wonder how fast I can be fired again— it's real good what I did," he continued, and he walked out of his house at eight o'clock in the a.m., proudly strutting his drooping flesh.

The air was sewn thick with the hilarity of his neighbors.

His car did not start, and so he began to walk down the street, embarrassed by the silly clothes the gawking people wore. "Have they no dignity?" he said to himself. "And I thought I was prudish; well, sure, I am now," and he stood upright and thrust out his soft, sagging white chest and sauntered down the hot sidewalk, proffering haughty glances to outraged citizens. A black and white patrol car soon pulled alongside him.

The two officers, stretching their black polyester uniforms to the breaking point with their burly forms, approached Rappal with the calm of men accompanied by an undeniable assurance of victory. "Citizen," the elder officer began, "is there a problem?"

Rappal's tilting brain was still able to recognize the historic colors and patterns of the police officers' clothes, thus allowing their entrance into his sinking world. "The world's gone mad—upside down, officers. People are walking around clothed in public!"

"We have clothes," said the younger officer, positioning himself next to his intended victim.

"Sure, well, right, that's good," Rappal said, his eyes blinking rapidly, his face frowning at this dilemma. "You need to wear clothes to show everyone who you are so you can arrest those crazy people who are breaking the law."

"Aren't we," the elder officer asked, calmly, looking askance at his younger partner, a signal to come around the offender, "breaking the law?"

"Well, no, you are the law, right?" he said. "I mean, you have to show the people who you are—geez," and he smiled, feeling good about his answer.

"Above the law, eh?"

Rappal's ambitious smile fell into a freezing lake of distress. "You're lawbreakers too, then," he cried, releasing the powerful rage that plowed down through his cluttered mind. He weaseled away from the officers and fled down the street, shouting thunderous admonitions. "The world's gone mad, the world's gone mad, mad, mad," and he turned the corner and disappeared into the deep density of the wild.

Once in the full embrace of the gnarled thicket, he peered over a landscape of multicolored foliage, and gazed at the distant dwellings of Man. "Animals, all of them disgusting animals," he whispered, and he looked round his bloodied self. "I wonder if my own kind might be here," and so he began to look about for allies. It was not too much time after this that he met one. "Hey, there, friend," he said, smiling, causing his new acquaintance to stop moving, "I'm home!"

Indeed, he made many entirely new friends that day and for many days thereafter, leading them on many expeditions through the verdant hills, teaching them the ways of the world, feeling their gratification all the while.

How attentive, how quiescent, how obedient his new friends were, so eager to learn the ways of the city dwellers.

"We are safe here," one of his admirers said, writhing its sleek body, "from them."

"They have no conscience," one of the taller ones with the furry red coat whispered in a weary voice.

"This is surely paradise," Rappal said, passionately, "so innocent."

"Liars and deceivers who will kill you for pleasure—them," barked a tan-colored, four-legged creature.

"Unknown," said the largest of Rappal's new family, one who sat on its haunches and gnawed at the sinewy hot air, "are they, here."

And so it was that Rappal became the Leader Supreme of these wild creatures because he walked upright and could reason and bring them power and organization they had never imagined.

* * * * *

The arrangement of the snakes into hunting packs brought a wealth of food to their scaly stomachs. "You belly sliders," Rappal called them, "will circulate in right circles and eat all you want, but you stay in that area." To the gray wolf, he promised a greater area to traverse. "You circulate in left circular patterns and eat all you want, but you furry four-legs must not eat the belly sliders." To the brown bear, he promised a grand sweep of the woods. "You giants can roam on the outside of the belly sliders and furry four-legs' hunting ground, and eat all you want, but not them," he said, smiling and clapping his hands.

And so it was under the reign of their King that these and other predators flourished as never before, multiplying in great numbers and diminishing their game with amazing rapidity. The great diversity of snakes cleaned their territory in thirty days' time, the wolves ravaged their area of all game in twenty days, and the bears gorged themselves on their tiny enemies until none was left within four weeks.

At the Great Council, the Representatives of the snakes and wolves and bears and coyotes—the foxes and falcons and the owls and eagles refused to attend, as all of them considered themselves above and beyond this finite ritual—were present before their King to argue their case for expanding their territories.

"You need boundaries, geez," Rappal said, exasperated, his purple rage beginning to bubble and foam in his hot brain. "You're predators, you eat flesh," and he grabbed his own darkened skin, "flesh, you can't go around eating each other and be happy, and you can't eat each other's food either—geez," he moaned, massaging his purple-as-an-eggplant face as he sat on a throne that had been hewn by his most voracious subjects. The throne was made of plant fiber, carefully spun by his humble servants, and while he sat on the matted seat of chaparral twine, his admirers danced about the magnificent amber-colored, vermilion-soaked, thatched structure. His oily, gravelly voice, to them, seared the ripe summer air with a tincture of sweet, fragrant honey-blossoms, and hatched a bubbly buoyancy in their enthralled little insect and animal bodies.

"We are many," the king diamondback hissed, lying, coiled up, atop his inferior ranks; "our bellies are empty."

"The Old Ways call us," the brown bear growled, his enormous, chocolate-colored head rocking to and fro as he sat on his powerful haunches.

"The Old Ways!" Rappal cried, astonished, compelling his tiny worshippers around him to momentarily halt their wild antics. "Competing for food all the time—geez! That makes small families, and that's no good—everyone knows big families are best; more variety, you know, I mean, if one dies, another takes his spot. Look, if one of you gets eaten, you have to have a replacement so everyone doesn't cry all day."

The coyote congregation embraced this philosophy, howling wildly, while the snakes hissed disapproval.

"I have heard it said," the black-striped snake hissed, "Man is descended from the Forest, that the Green Bush and the Giant Flesh Eater gave birth to him," and he fell upon his slender belly and crawled away amidst the uproar.

"Stupid, really stupid," Rappal, Prince of the Forest, replied, smiling a smile of contempt. "Man didn't come from all of you—we created all of you to serve us, everyone knows that; look." He raised his fat, brown hand up, flat. "Man is here," and he let his hand down abruptly, "plants and animals here." He was spewing righteousness as his subjects grew morose.

"Say you, we are beneath your naked foot?" said the gray wolf, his pointed ears pulled back.

"I am your King," Rappal demanded, "you listen to me, you obey me."

"No," the wolf replied, "we hear you only."

"Hear me?" and he began his rage, his bloated, deeply engrained, sunburnt face grimacing and frowning. "I speak, you obey—geez."

It seemed that all of the attendants expanded in size and moved toward him with the slow locomotion of a single organism.

Rappal felt a roaring cold chill frost his skin, and he felt the bald terror of a burgeoning imagination spit on his brain. "I mean 'obey' like friends obey each other, of course—we're friends, sure—I mean, friends obey each other, you know, like if one says 'let's go somewhere,' and the other agrees, it's obeying, but they're equals, sure, right—equal all the time," and he began to feel better and calmer as he settled down his own anxiety. Consequently, he saw this effect a gentler temper in his subjects, who let fall their erect hairs and let their tense, fierce bodies relax, and so he kept up his discursive dialogue, expiating into various veins of illogic and abstract ideas and perking their ears with an inflammatory pearl formed here, an incendiary gem there. "So," he gurgled, forgetting all the previous statements that were now lost in the hot mist of the fragrant garden, "we need to sacrifice a flesh eater to make the Forest god happy." For a moment he let this cup of gall spill into their gaping mouths; then, realizing his error, he made haste and feigned a continuous statement. "A Forest god," he said, and he raised his arms on high, "we don't know but demands worship—all worship." He reasoned that worshipping the Forest god before them would make him look humble and equal before this salivating throng.

"Whence did this god spring into our midst?" cried the spotted owl, who had been stealthily creeping into the camp and listening to this waxen verbiage. Even the voles, the owls' main diet, were found to utter low gasps in response to this query.

"Why, he's everywhere," Rappal replied, constructing a play upon his face wherein the players changed costume in every scene, "he's been here forever."

"Who is he?" the eagle demanded, sweeping down to rest upon the thick limb of a hearty sycamore tree.

"Who knows?" he said. "He could be anyone—you, for instance, I don't know—even me, maybe," and he sensed their rising irritation again. "But no, not me—geez," and he smiled nervously. "I know I'm not some god—but maybe our friend the brown bear or the owl there or that big oak tree is a god—who knows, huh?"

"Who do we sacrifice, eh?" the badger shouted, his black, furry back rising as he spied his natural enemies around him.

The entire group, as if still possessing a single mind, moved in closer toward Rappal.

"Well, I don't know, I don't want to talk, but the snakes have been saying that the badger needs to be sacrificed; I don't know, that's just what I heard, maybe…" Rappal's natural defense rose up as quickly as a flash flood in summer.

As the concept of lying did not exist in the animal and insect kingdoms, the snakes began to hiss and writhe over themselves, secreting pheromones of danger, exciting the crowd to a frenzy; Rappal's torrent of mistruths had bewildered the animals, and now this accusation took hold of their primitive brains, and all of them began to emit their individual howl of displeasure, creating a madhouse of rhapsody in screeching violet.

Rappal's face took on that particular shade of panic when dark shadows prey upon a boasting liar, and he said, "Well, maybe it was the badger or the wolf," and he rambled on until the pitch of protestations and the creeping movement of the creatures toward him finally broke his desire. "All right, no sacrifice, then; whatever you want is best, of course. I mean, who needs gods, right?"

He felt the first sting on his naked right calf, the pinch of the deadly yellow scorpion, and the other pinches were indistinguishable as he fell from the throne onto the mass of decaying plants.

"He is Man," the owl said, hooting loudly as he dug his claws into Rappal's numb scalp, "we are safe here, but Man invades us. We know now who this one is."

"Far from Man," the animals chanted, amassing atop Rappal.

"We will show Man, now," the owl said.

And so it all began.

It took exactly one year to transform Rappal.

The animals created a new species, taking out Rappal's organs and glands and building new ones; the new species was slowly created when his bone marrow and blood were sucked dry and his bones were eaten by greedy insects and his ruddy skin gobbled up by bacteria and fungus. An original life-form took shape as they installed appropriate life-giving mechanisms.

All the organisms of the Forest waited patiently while the bear finally removed the covering of fiber that shrouded the new creature, and then the animals danced around the latest inhabitant of the Forest, celebrating, squealing in glee, each taking a turn to properly mark it with their unique scent.

In truth it was more like a tree, due to its large, cylindrical red trunk burrowing into the rich, black soil; yet, the trunk was human tissue and sinew, encased in cellulose, and was soft to the touch. In its nucleus was Rappal's heart, pumping the red liquid of life through his numerous veins, which were enclosed in a root-like structure that sank deep into the earth to absorb the dense nutrients. The limbs were arteries enwrapped in woody cellulose fiber and brown bark, limbs that were gnarled and twisted around as if in agony; yet sprouting from each thick limb was a head of Rappal, and each head was filled with a sugary pulp that fed the indigenous wildlife.

The large vermilion heads with the squishy serpentine veins popping out from their foreheads could talk. Sometimes the animals of the Forest would sit and listen to the stories the heads told. "Geez, come on, I don't have to be your leader, all right?" one of the heads would begin, while another head was already on its way to another lie. "I'm in charge here, understand? Raccoons eat on Mondays only, that's important." And still another head simply cried tears of red juice, while another head bargained for its release as long as it betrayed the other heads. The animals loved this story time, and often they would suck on the tree's delicious sap afterward and laugh heartily as the heads cried out in pain. Birds would land upon the fat limbs and pick at the heads to savor their sweet meat. "Eat him," one of the heads would cry out in terror, "over there, he tastes better! The bluebird told me so!" "Liar! Liar!" the other heads would reply. "He's the tastiest!"

The day of the creature's debut as a life-form, all the organisms of the Forest lent their ear to the sagacious words of the master of this ceremony. "This is the hallowed spot where She fell," began the great spotted owl, and the congregation struck a solemn repose, lying prostrate upon the cool, lumpy,

wet soil, "She who fed us and mended our wounds and protected us from encroachment by Man."

"She," the multitudes sang, "saved us from the treachery
of Them."

"She fell here, her blood bathed the land, here," the owl
continued, turning his noble head askance, "and it is only right
that the New Life be created here to honor Her Great Life."

"It is right and good," the devotees to Her memory
murmured.

"For Her memory, we will give the New Life a chance to
be its old life if it does not speak those things which do not
exist; the merciful Forest will give him life or give him unlife."

"Who," said all of the frowning Rappal heads, "who,
who, who…"

"To return to the old life, the New Life must not speak
things which do not exist for one full cycle of the silver ball to
the next," continued the owl, "and he will have one full cycle
of the seasons in which to do this. It is only fair." His raised
his noble face high and waited for dissension, but there was
none. "He will also become that animal which he offends if
he speaks those things which do not exist, and this will add
one more going up and coming down of the yellow mother
in the sky onto his sentence to free himself."

"No problem," one of Rappal's heads proclaimed, "one
month, sure, that's fair; yes, all right."

Two whole days transpired and Rappal's heads were listening to the teasing of the young red foxes. "O, great wormhead,"
a sly male began, snuggled next to his mate, "tell us how you
once ruled the Wild."

"I ain't no wormhead," one of the babbling heads retorted,
blushing with scarlet anger, "you need respect, and I did too
rule all the animals—hey, I was a Prince, loved by everyone

until I didn't want to rule anymore, not really. I wanted to see what it was like to be a tree and have birds eat your brains."

Now, his head had begun to transform these past two days back to its human self, but with this silly fabrication, he lost the Homo sapiens shape and instead, the head that lied became the face of a fox.

For many months the metamorphosis transpired, and visitors would sit and gaze, bemused, at the innocent coyote face sprouting from one of the limbs, or the fierce bear countenance or the handsome wolf's visage or any of a hundred other creatures Rappal had deceived. In the twelfth month, Rappal had gone twenty-nine days without lying and his human form was nearly complete, and his joy was abounding, his victory certain, his freedom assured.

"Tell us of Man's World," bellowed the great tortoise as he raised his spongy, wrinkled neck over the throngs who watched the continuing transformation. All of the animals of the Forest were there.

Rappal, conjoined with truth for so long, hesitated at first to narrate his past violations of the outside to this throng, but he admitted his life into the court of evidence; and the animals did not speak nor move, nay, they merely sat, like the white rabbit, or lay, like the coyote, or stood, like the red fox, all of them unable to tame their rising sentiment of terror.

The circumference of the emotional violence he had wrought upon his fellow creatures radiated beyond him and into the audience. The expanding concentric waves of this pure hatred Rappal had felt toward his own kind peeled off from its malignant radius and sowed a creepy, crawling image into the animals' minds.

He, Rappal, who continued to move toward full physical humanness again, came to his history at the restaurant, and when he mentioned one particular name, all the creatures lay prostrate in reverence.

"Lauren," all of the creatures whispered, worshipfully. "She," they uttered, weeping, "She saved us from the Terror."

All the sparkling pink hues drained from Rappal's changing face. It had been eerie for him to produce the truth these past months, and he had, in his numerous heads, often thought of the value and consequences of speaking the truth. He had never been able to reconcile in his mind whether or not imparting the truth was beneficial in any manner except for freeing himself from this exile.

"You knew the Lauren," sang the owl. "Tell us about the Great She."

Rappal's large pumpkin head shook and his face turned ashen white when he finally understood that it was Lauren who had died upon the very spot where he was now fastened into the ground. To lie now would doom him forever, he knew, but to tell the Truth would incur the wrath of every living creature in this majestic and enigmatic Forest. He began to tell the Truth of it all, truly he did, even coloring every despicable crime against Lauren with lucid pictures, and he thought this blunt honesty would appease his captors; but, nay, they became incensed, and began to move toward him, uttering weird, guttural noises.

Rappal, knowing he was so close to consummation, began to tremble, and sap began to run down his trunk legs. "Geez, I was just saying all that to see if you really did like Lauren; what a gal she was, really, I treated her like a queen, really, she was the best; sure, I remember the time when she asked for time off to come up here to fight those developers, and I said, 'You bet, Lauren, can I come, too?' and she said, 'Sure,' but, you know, I had to stay and run the store—yeah, Lauren, what a wonderful girl," and he began to weep as the scowling creatures retreated, which encouraged him to continue his imaginative embroidery. "Lauren, so giving, so kind—I offered her a position as assistant manager, but, you know, she wanted to move on and help people all over the world." Why, he wondered, agitated, did he hear heavy echoes now of his greasy voice?

His giant pumpkin head, cranked around, beheld the budding of more Rappal heads, and saw his giant head in the nucleus of the tree dwindling, and he began to scream a scream resembling that of an animal being eaten alive. Now, he felt his consciousness stream through the forming arteries into the new heads, which began to babble, some lying, some truthful, some imploring mercy, others arguing with each other.

The time of one year came up a moment later, and the entire affair came to a conclusion. Rappal was soon no more as his heads were eaten by voracious red ants and vindictive blue jays, the heads screaming all the while and attempting to weave new tales to placate their tormentors.

When it was all over, the animals and insects of the Forest sat in awe as they stared at the unparalleled Epiphany, a pristine image created by the last creature Rappal had offended. There, in the slender brown trunk of this unfurling tree, in the strong, curvaceous limbs and yellow, bright blossoms, in the red and green, crisp leaves that swayed in the warm wind, was the image of a sublime figure, a woman of natural strength and effortless grace and original beauty.

This eternal flame of courage and ebullient kindness was the delicate form of She.

Born that wondrous day was the hallowed Lauren Tree.

-Finis-

Animal Stories

There was a crème-colored sports utility vehicle traveling down a dark, serpentine highway. In this brand-new, state-of-the-art, built-like-an-army-tank automobile were four human beings—a father, who was young and smart and eager for this trip; a mother, who was young and smart and who also was eager for this journey to the magical artistry of Yosemite; and then there were the two children, a darling girl who was eight years old and full of life and full of love for all creatures and who imagined this trip like going into a beautiful dream, and finally, the youngest member of the family, a boy of only five, who considered any event that took him out of his carefully controlled and monitored environment to be as great a journey just as if he and his family were going to the moon; and there was no sin in the boy or the girl, as sin relates to the kind of sophisticated, well-thought-out, chronic sin that grown-ups indulge in, but the normal kind of mischievous play, silly play, the normal energetic buoyancy of a growing mind that makes ordinary, honest mistakes and practices regular contrition because it does not yet have that awful capacity to hold a grudge forever and still seeks to be happy; to be exact, the children were more like angelic creatures, and everyone who met them thought so. The parents were sweet and kind and loving too, and had a particular fondness for animals, and no stray cat or dog ever suffered once this family saw them; and as a family, they took regular trips to the zoo and to the mountains to appreciate the legacy of this planet's spectacular foliage and fauna.

Mr. Father was proud of the fact that he had never, not ever, not once struck a cat or dog on the road, and not even a bird or snake or coyote; not any living, large creature had he ever hit, and he prayed often that he might never, ever hit one, too; but Mrs. Mom had not been so fortunate, and once she had struck a crazed dog in her neighborhood—the kind who attacks your car as you drive—even though she had expertly swerved to avoid the adorable Shih Tzu; but, alas, she had hit it and then—thump—she had run right over its small black-and-white-haired body with the front wheels of her big sedan, and even before she had exited the car she was nauseous, and even before she beheld the squished but still squiggling canine, she was weeping, and even before she was back in her car, she was calling her husband to grieve with him. It was her husband who carried the dying mutt—with the same sorrow and horror of a man holding a dead boy—to the house of the neighbor who had kept the dog sealed up in her house like it was sometimes a handsomely stuffed toy and other times like it was a small creature that did not need anything other than what she needed; and as he presented the lifeless body to the neighbor woman, she somehow understood the pain of the killer and her accomplice and actually wept with the husband and wife and embraced them and later became good friends with them.

Husband and wife never drove over fifteen miles per hour in their neighborhood after that disturbing event.

Well, here were the animal lovers and their near-inno-
cent children singing merry songs and playing road games
like "don't complete the word" and "twenty questions," and
laughing and smiling, and eating savory, warm food, when
Mrs. Animal—or was it Ms.?—suddenly appeared directly in
the path of the family vehicle and just stood there and stared
blankly at the fast-coming object.

Mr. Father and honorable Husband swerved, and hard too,
way to the left, a sharp, very quick turn, so sharp that, yes,
the front wheels obeyed being violently yanked and so slipped
into a new direction but unfortunately could not deliver an
important message to their master at the steering wheel—that
the angle and new course achieved were too sudden and not
to be overcome—and so the tires, coerced to obey the simple
laws of physics, took a short skid, sucking the back tires along
for the ride, and thus the front end of the car began to rise
up and began to roll, over and over and over again in a nasty
pounding of metal and asphalt and fiery sparks of broken glass
until the small, crushed-like-a-tin-can-for-the-sake-of-the-
dumb-animal utility vehicle came to a sickening, slow halt
and morbid thud; and then, boom, an uncomfortable quiet
was achieved, where there should have been merriment and
joy and the noise of a family living.

The brown-and-red-spotted deer with the small, wet black
nose walked over to the funny-looking object with the two
high-beam headlights still on and the black rubber tires still
spinning and the eerie silence from within the metallic hull
of the sideways-leaning structure, and very politely and very
carefully reached up and placed its two hard front hooves on
the side door and then very softly lifted up its right foot and
placed it on the window of the passenger seat and tapped,
tapped, tapped very, very softly and then said, very much in

earnest, and not at all in jest, as no respectable deer in good standing would ever boast at an indelicate time such as this, "O humans," it purred, "I thank thee for thy sacrifice to save mine life, for thou hast once more taught us that we are equal brothers with thee," and it was teary-eyed too, at least the best it could as a way of imitating humans it had studied, "and so, I bid you adieu, and a blessed sleep," and the saddened animal trotted toward the "deer crossing" sign and then jumped gaily into the deep, dark, creepy forest.

Now, this is the first of the animal stories, where we meet our little animal friends and are invited to share their thoughts on matters near and dear to their small hearts; and so, here now is the second story for your entertainment!

Story * * * * * the Second

"Mama," the son said to his mother as he worked on his essay, "what are 'humble origins'?"

"Son," replied the proud Mother, "it is a time to think about where we came from and what we are grateful for today."

The son tilted his curly-haired blonde head and a thoughtful expression caressed his dark face. "And what do we have today, Mama?"

Mama smiled affectionately. "We have a roof over our heads, plenty of good food to eat, and our health—we have much to be grateful for, little one."

The son scrunched up his small face and placed his head on the front end of the sofa. "I think I know what to write now, Mama," he said, and so he went to work.

When his essay was completed, he read it to his beloved Mother.

"'Dear Poor People Around the World, Whoever and Wherever You Are,'" he began, and then said to his Mama, "isn't that right, to begin this way, because I don't even know their names?"

"Yes, dear."

He smiled and nodded his shaggy head, and continued. "'I just want to thank you for allowing our benefactor to spend so much money on our kin.' Gosh, Mama, I don't know what else to write about."

"Well, son, you might tell them that you are thankful that our benefactor has such a good, good heart, and that she cares for all creatures equally—not one above the other, not our mistress." She watched carefully as her son wrote down a few more sentences, and then she continued in her fervent tone. "She, after all, sends money every month not to these poor people but to our poor relations so they might have a place to stay and be adopted, as we were." She paused again and watched as her child fumbled with the yellow pencil between his spongy, black, padded paws. "And every month she has our toenails manicured, our teeth cleaned, our hair done, and when your father died—bless his rotting carcass—she hired a psychologist for me so I might properly lessen my grief—all good money that could easily have gone to starving humans but instead went to us—mere dogs, as some unsympathetic humans call us—but our mistress has happily re-made us in her own image—mere humans—by treating us like herself; why, just look at my diamond necklace, my cashmere sweater, my perfumed fur—so wonderful!"

The silly poodle son rolled over onto his back and wriggled about. "I like living with our mistress; she lets us walk on the dinner table and eat with her and she doesn't even get mad when I do my business on the rug—she is fun!"

"Yes, child, she treats us right—now, finish your letter, so we can mail it to those poor, poor people who are starving to death but somehow don't seem to mind that their fellow humans are spending great amounts of money on dogs and not them; I think," she said, thoughtfully, "it will make them feel better if they knew that many humans who have extra money don't just spend it on frivolous matters, but on creatures who benefit from it—like us—and so I do think they would feel better knowing at least someone is happier because of the generosity of people like our good mistress."

"Yeah!" the male poodle barked, "for poor people!"

A week hence, a family, living in a hut of yellow straw and bamboo leaves, and starving on a diet of rusty water and cold soup gleaned from yellowing grass and a few grains of stale rice, received a letter; the grossly emaciated mother tried to open it but had not the strength to do so, and so she passed it to the family strongman, her husband, who barely managed to rip the sweetly scented, exquisitely designed envelope apart.

"What is it, Father?" the wife asked, feeling too weak to even look at the fallen contents of the envelope.

Father, using his skinny fingers, retrieved the fine stationery and turned it over, only to reveal a series of eerie squiggles and uneven strokes of pencil markings that rose up and down the page in a meandering, zigzag, upside-down pattern. "I do not know, Mama, it has no alphabet, at all—and I am familiar with at least some letters—and there are no letters here, to be sure."

"But look, Papa," said their daughter in a tiny, weak, inflamed voice, who was ten years old but looked six due to malnourishment and the horrible ravages of unfettered disease, "a picture," and she now seemed weaker for the speaking of it.

"A picture," said the father, and picked it up to reveal the portrait of two pampered-looking bleach-blondes, dressed in ostentatious finery and sporting a weird smile on their bulbous faces.

Mama smiled. "I could eat dog," she whispered, rubbing her aching, swollen belly.

"Dog would be good for two weeks," Father said, licking his dry, bloody lips.

"Do you think someone means to send us these dogs so we might eat them?" asked the girl in a barely audible whisper.

"One can only hope," said the Mother, inspecting the expensive jewelry on the animals, "that we could have anything in this picture, so we might live another day."

The intensity of the sun intruded rudely upon the hopes of the family, and soon they were lying on the hard desert floor again, waving away the black hordes of flies and brushing away the insects as they had done for so long now, but now they were dreaming of fresh meat and a way home again.

The next day they found their way home, by dying.

This completes the second of the animal stories, which may be rendered as horror to some and weird tales to others; yet do not let this dissuade you from partaking in the next and last story, which has been designed purposely to amuse a certain species of sentient creatures.

Story the * * * * * Third

She was born and raised on a farm, so it was only natural that she would witness the singular relationship between man and animal in such an environment; and it soon became apparent to her parents that the young girl had a deep affection for animals and abhorred the way they were treated on the farm. She was a pretty child and very bright and passionate about harm that was done to every inhabitant of Nature, so when she adopted a philosophy that opposed the harming of any animal, and refused to eat animal flesh or drink their milk or wear their skins, her parents, although they did not agree with her, understood it. When she was only twelve years old, she visited the homes of every farmer in the valley and secured signatures from them for a petition and then presented it to the mayor and city council and watched with pride as they passed a new law to monitor sanitary conditions at the local slaughterhouses.

As she grew older, her passion to protect animals grew too, her ideas on how to protect them evolved, and the list of creatures, both wild and domestic, that she wanted to be protected expanded. When she was in high school, the flax-en-haired, slender beauty with the emerald green eyes united with two classmates to investigate the way a local university was using monkeys for its medical research and exposed the cruel acts done to these animals, and because of this inquiry, the research lab was shut down and the monkeys were taken away to a local zoo. It seemed as if she were finding her true calling in life and that nothing now could stop her.

She looked around the world and realized that there were few organizations that existed to protect the welfare of animals. "So, I shall create one," she said to her fiancé, "and I shall call it "Animals Are People, Too—or AAPT." And then, using American Sign Language, she signed the new name. Her fiancé kissed her and praised her, and married her because of her unbridled fervor to treat all living things as equals. She was now Lindsay Travers, wife of Seth Travers, and now they would not be stopped.

Together, they broke into research laboratories the world over and videotaped the test animals and released the disturb-ing images to the press. Where there were animals abused, they were there; they were there in small boats on rough seas protesting foreign sailors in foreign ships that hunted whales, but could do nothing but weep as the gentle giants of the seas lay dying in their death throes before their very teary eyes; they were there scrutinizing companies that used animals for product testing, and they compelled many such companies to ban such practices; they were there when men with big wooden clubs went hunting for white-furred baby seals, and they turned these men away and won court rulings against this barbaric practice. Wherever there was gross negligence in the case of how humans handled animals, they were there, and when the AAPT was much older and much braver, Lindsay and Seth looked beyond the mission statement of the organization, which was, "We are here to serve and protect all animals, whom we consider precious and equal and our friends," and decided that they had only begun.

"For now," Lindsay stated at a meeting of the executive board, which was followed by signing the name of their organization, "we must not only protect, but liberate our animal friends." Thus, the organization began to break into research facilities and free the caged animals.

There was a time when they broke into a university research lab and liberated hundreds of lab rats and then chained themselves to the doors of the place as they awaited the press and the police. "We have freed our brethren from servitude," Lindsay announced, smugly, to the anxious reporters.

But one of the research assistants, after observing the damage done to her facility, stood before Lindsay as the police were about to lead her away. "What have you done, you," she said, her face blanched with shock, "what have you done, you dangerous, vile creature, you, who holds the life of rodents above the life and needs of Man; you," she shook her head, "what damage you have done to help those who cannot walk, cannot move their hands," and she slowly lifted up her hands, "to those who cannot hold their loved ones," and she thrust out her arms as if to embrace someone, "for creatures not human, not human at all…"

Lindsay smirked, then smiled, and laughed, and then said, as if she were addressing a most uncommon criminal, "You can't just torture innocent creatures for your impossible schemes—you can't play god with creatures simply because you deem them inferior to you; shame, shame on you!" And as she worked herself into a righteous fury, and began to chant, "Free the slaves, free the prisoners," so too did her fellow conspirators, in the same manner people from time immemorial have protested the inhumane treatment of human slaves and prisoners—with great passion and force, so much so that they would, had the moment demanded it, have laid down their lives for their brown, furry, large friends, who even now were romping aimlessly through the local verdant fields, and who, had they been given human thought even for a brief stroke of time, would have rushed pell-mell and happily jumped back into their sturdy steel cages and subjected themselves to every poke and needle and experiment.

"But even this is not enough," Lindsay later decided, "for such people who run these places are criminals, and they are enslaving our own, and do not suffer for their sins." Thus, the organization took to bombing places that would not relent in their testing of animals, and even bombing those places that did stop such practices. "We must teach those who break the law that they will be punished for what they have done—just as a person who commits a crime is punished even if he admits his guilt and repents." Money now poured in from celebrities who lived in the upper tiers of society and who knew no hardship or suffering but somehow had an inexplicably close relationship with creatures that did not possess any species of thought. "Now, we are famous, and have much weight in the world," she cried, in front of many microphones and television cameras, and after signing the name of her organization, she said with great pride, "and you shall know our name." She felt invincible, just as warring nation-states of old did when first they picked up the hammer and sickle to attack their defenseless neighbors.

Now, wherever there was any threat to animals, the AAPT sought to be there; they targeted a seafood restaurant that killed lobsters by boiling them alive, decrying this practice by stating that these poor crustaceans, imprisoned in their watery dungeon, sat defenseless and humiliated as customers mocked them and lusted after their flesh. "And then these innocent creatures of the sea are boiled alive, and have their limbs torn from them and then sliced to pieces, and all the while they wail in agony, just like you and I would under the knife of any inhuman butcher," thus spoke Lindsay, in her most condemning tone and attacking posture.

The owner of the restaurant appeared outside during the protest, smiling all the while, dressed in his bloodstained chef's apron and munching on a juicy, red lobster's leg, and then boasting that his cash register was overflowing due to all this publicity; and then turning to his antagonists, he invited them back next week to protest the handling of the frozen fish in his deep-freeze lockers. "We do not coddle them, to be sure," he began, with a mischievous gleam in his periwinkle eyes; "no, no, I figure that since they are dead, they won't mind, really—and sometimes we throw them from cook to cook, but we never drop them," he said, wagging his finger, "we are very good with our hands," and held his up, smiling like the boy who has caught the golden goose. Lindsay lunged at the man, but was held back by her husband, and she vowed to return to this place she deemed a slaughterhouse with court orders to investigate the mistreatment of any of her "beautiful children."

"Animals should not be caged or kept in homes or backyards," Lindsay later declared at a meeting of the press in front of many cameras and microphones, after first signing the name of her organization in front of the restaurant, "for they were never meant to be our slaves, and they should all be wild and free again, as Nature intended them to be; so, I am against humans owning pets of any kind; and now I even oppose the killing of insects, for insects have as much a right to life as animals, and I will not even kill a spider or a fly, and I watch where I walk to make sure no creature dies because of my negligence and arrogance." Indeed, one of her loyal adjutants now carried a broom and brushed the sidewalk in front of her wherever she went, and she wore plugs in her nose and plugs in her ears, so that she might not accidentally inhale or entrap an "Innocent."

She secretly endorsed the burning down of establishments that did not adhere to her strict code of ethics in the treatment of animals, and soon her organization was actively participating in the burning of clinics that did not adhere to their dogma. Once, an employee in one of the testing laboratories died, and after one of Lindsay's own faithful was sent to prison for this, she turned to Seth and said, rather matter-of-factly, "This is war, and our own might suffer, and soldiers die."

They protested any company that sold furs and any company that sold milk and any company that sold meat and any company that sold any animal product and any company that sold any material that was gained from the carcass of a dead animal; to wit, they protested against nearly every company on the entire planet. "We war against the savages who seek to destroy our friends," she declared to her own, "and we will brook no failure."

She was having another one of her conferences where all the press were clamoring for her speech, and after she had signed the name of her organization, one of the reporters asked the following question, "Ms. Travers, I understand that you grant human rights to all creatures, but I must ask you, where do you stop? What about the common bacteria you are stepping on just now, and the germs you wiped out when last you took penicillin—or will you never leave your house for fear of killing a bacterium and never receive medicine even when you are very ill; and what about dangerous animals, Ms. Travers, what if a poisonous snake were in your daughter's crib or a bear was about to attack your child or a rabid dog was about to bite your husband? What then, Lindsay, what then, and where do you go from here, since you seem to have gone everywhere from where you first began?"

Lindsay smiled arrogantly and looked the male reporter up and down, just as if she were deciding whether or not he should in fact live past the next hour. "There are no such things as wild animals, only animals we have made wild with our incessant hunting and torturing of them; and as for the question of the bacteria, I do not feel they are sentient creatures, therefore they do not qualify as a protected species; and no, Mr. Smart-aleck-reporter-man, I would never, ever," and she raised up her index finger and wagged it in his face, "ever kill an animal under any circumstances, any more than I would kill a human being if I felt he was a threat to me." She smiled now, knowing the whole world was watching, and then said in a pleasing, demure and feminine voice, "Animals, they are just like people, and they are all very gentle and loving, if you would just give them a chance." She then paused, and said solemnly, "All creatures that feel pain deserve the right to live."

The reporter was undaunted. "So, why don't you and your husband go camping in the wild and live with the bears and mountain lions and show us how it is all done and win us over?"

Seth was standing right next to his beloved wife, and he leaned over and said, quite smoothly and assuredly, "We will," and held up the hands of his wife as the people around them cheered.

They clearly had no intent to stay in the mountains longer than a week, as they knew that no one in the press, who were on the periphery of this camp, would stay longer than that, but a curious thing happened while Lindsay and Seth took long walks in the woods, holding hands, and simply sat and observed the sublime theater of Nature—they found themselves in love with the doctrine they had been preaching. "We have been talking about Nature but we have never truly been in her sacred bosom," she said to Seth, "so, here we will make our abode."

Seven months later, and it was late October, and they were still there, having decided that the AAPT was part of another life, another layer they had peeled off so they might see a greater truth that was hidden from their "city eyes." They drove their jeep into town for supplies and never stayed too long because they did not want to be too far removed or too long away from the precious animals they had recently adopted.

"I will name this one Sarah Jean," Lindsay said one early morning as she stood on a hill with her husband, as she stared at the great black bear that was munching on a large, pink salmon.

"And I will name the male Chuck," said Seth, and held the slender hand of his wife as they observed the two bears explore the edge of the riverbed.

It was not too much later that the two humans had acquired the trust of the bear families in these high mountains, and they were even able to sit amid the bears without being molested, as some human observers have done with gorilla families. "Once we were preachers of the word about Nature, and now we are proponents of it," whispered Lindsay as she watched in fascination as the mother bear, Sarah Jean, cradled and cuddled her newborn cub, Junior; "when we go back, we will be greater than ever, for we will be authentic."

One day in town, two of the local farmers came up to the couple and spoke to them in grave terms. "We have had a sparse season 'round these parts, and I know you people are cozy up there with them bears, but they might be getting hungry this winter 'cause of the slim pickings 'n' all, and I wouldn't get too close to them…"

"If'n I was you," finished the other elderly gentleman.

"Well, thank you for your concern," responded Lindsay in her politest tone.

"If you folks do decide on staying up there, I might suggest you purchase a firearm of some considerable force, and some kind of mean one, too," said the first farmer.

"If'n you want to live, that is," finished the other gentleman.

"No, thank you," replied Seth; "we do not believe in murdering animals for any reason; we live with them and treat them as equals."

The first farmer rubbed his white beard and thought a spell upon this boast, and then said, nodding his head, "Bears ain't human, and ain't too particular what they eat when they is hungry, be it friend or foe, and they certainly have had human dinner guests before."

"And the humans weren't eating nothing, if'n you get my drift," said the other gentleman, winking.

"Thank you for your concern, but we will do just fine without slaughtering Nature's creatures," said Lindsay, and she and Seth walked away and drove back up to their campground and walked to their tents and enjoyed a good meal and made plans for the future.

"Of course, we will have to find a cabin to stay in during the winter," Seth said to his wife, "and then we will come back in early spring."

"Why? Do the bears leave and come back? Why must we? Humans and animals coexisted peacefully for thousands of years until we started hunting them, and now they fear us and naturally fight back against us; if our ancestors lived here, so can we—and besides, if we leave now, will we not lose all that we have gained?"

But her husband knew better than to argue with her now, for when she posed such questions, it meant that her mind was firm on the proposal, and so he bought provisions to stay on through a very cold and snowy winter.

It was late November now and the cold rains were coming and the temperature was falling faster at night and not rising much during the day. Lindsay, much to the relief of Seth, decided that indeed they should find a cabin and come back in the early spring. "But we must bid farewell to our trusted comrades," she said, and Seth heartily agreed, and so the two of them walked hand in hand toward the place where the bear families congregated, and stood there and watched the frolicking bears, and then vacated the site.

Two months later, they were back in their black jeep, desperate to visit their good friends, the black bears of these high mountains. "We are back," Lindsay cried, approaching the familiar site where her bears lived, but then she stopped short. "Seth, just look at Sarah Jane and Chuck, they look so thin, the poor things."

"The poor things," Seth said, grimacing now as he studied the situation. "Maybe we ought not to have come back now, maybe the farmers were right."

"Oh, phooey on the farmers—the bears are our friends, for goodness' sake," she said, and looking out toward the meadow, she shouted, "Chuck, Sarah Jane, and Junior—you little sweetie—it's us, your human family!" and she held up a great big bag of blueberries and began waving it about.

"I am beginning to think that bringing these berries was a mistake, too," Seth said, nervously, as he watched the bears stand up on their hind paws and sniff the ripe air with their big, wet, black, wiggling noses.

"Oh, don't be silly," Lindsay said, waving his remark away, and still looking toward the bears; "come and get it, come and get your gift from us," and she continued to jog the sweet berries up and down, up and down, and she was still smiling with glee when the bears came prancing on all fours toward her.

"Let's get out of here, Lindsay," Seth said, his voice full of trepidation, and his body trembling like a thin reed in the wind.

"Oh, would you stop, you silly goose!" she cried, smiling still as the bears were fast approaching.

Seth grabbed her firmly by the arm and attempted to pull her back toward the jeep, but she simply pulled away from him and actually walked toward the galloping bears; he was beaten, he knew he was, and so he decided to follow her, as he always had, and proceeded to walk behind her. "Sorry, babe, I just panicked for a moment."

"Oh, don't worry about a thing…" Lindsay began, but her next words then stopped in her spastic throat and seemed to cut her and bleed down to her stomach, where she felt as if she had indeed swallowed shards of sharp glass, for she had just then looked up into the howling, foaming, black cauldron of untamed and unbound Nature and inhaled the acrid smoke of a primitive mind and magnificent body that knew no reason or bore no good will toward any living thing and that obeyed an eternal mechanism for survival which spoke of killing anything and anyone that would aid its existence.

"Look, Mommy, dinner!" the Bear Cub cried to its mother as it ran toward the walking human meals.

"Just in time for supper," said Papa Bear, rising up on his fat haunches and letting loose a terrible roar as he opened his mouth full of yellowing daggers and lifted up his muscular arms and reached out with his awesome sharp claws to grab hold of the petrified prey.

"Now, Papa, don't be greedy, we haven't eaten in so long," Mama Bear said, gently scolding her husband.

"Pasghetti," Baby Bear ejaculated, as he watched Papa Bear rip into the tender, white meat and pull its stringy flesh apart.

"Not a struggle out of this one, so quiet, how nice for us," Mama Bear said to Baby Bear, digging in at the head of the corpse, "even though I know your father likes a good fight before he starts to eat."

When the family was close to finishing their delicious, albeit somewhat dry and saltless meal, Baby Bear, who was munching on the organs of the creature, noticed another object nearby, and said, his mouth dripping with red blood and warm guts, "Mama, what's that, what's that, it looks like food but it doesn't move like food?"

Mama Bear too raised her head and, upon staring at the prostrate figure, said, white skin and tissue hanging from her huge jowls, "Look, Papa, what do you make of that?"

Papa Bear looked up, gobs of blood decorating his snout, and spied the still object. "Hmm," he bellowed, and sauntered over to the object just as if he were in a smorgasbord restaurant and wanting another tasty dish; and when he reached the thing he smelled it and then moved it with his paws, but it seemed uninteresting.

"Papa, bite it, bite it," Baby Bear said, eagerly.

Papa Bear walked around to the head of the creature, which had long blonde hair and a ribbon in it, and he gave it a quick nip, and then heard, much to his surprise, a whimpering sound emanating from it. "Could it be alive, yet—another meal, perhaps? Are we so blessed, Mama?"

Mama came over and saw now that the slender, moving thing was trying to crawl away and hold up its fingers in curious signs but Papa Bear kept putting his massive paws on its body and occasionally biting it. "Perhaps it is trying to communicate to us, Papa," she said, curiously, and put her head toward the struggling thing, her hot breath blowing an ill wind, blood from her teeth dripping down onto the wet face of the babbling creature; "it is saying something, what do you think it is?"

Papa Bear feigned a concerned look, and said, in a whisper, "It is trying to say," and as he rose up, there erupted from him a terrible roar, "supper's on!" and he fell upon the whining, screeching thing and began to devour its cute, little, perfumed round head with a cacophony of violent crackling and crunching.

"Oh, Papa," Mama Bear returned, "always one to make fun!" and she too joined in on the feast, but when Baby Bear came to join in, he was turned away and admonished by his mother. "You must not leave the supper table until you have eaten every drop! Don't you know there are starving bears in the world, and what would they think if we let good meat go to waste?"

"Yes, Mama," Baby Bear replied, and dolefully went back to finish eating the carcass.

Papa Bear looked lovingly at Mama Bear, and Mama Bear looked lovingly at Papa Bear, and then she said, "Oh, come on, Baby, come and join us in this fresh kill! After all, the family that eats together plays together!"

As Baby Bear approached the still-twitching, gored and gnawed thing, he stopped and stared at it, and said, with surprising maturity, "But Mama, isn't this a human creature? Aren't we supposed to be their friends? And didn't these humans live here without harming us?"

Papa Bear lifted up his bloodied mouth and sat back heavily upon his haunches as he stared at his offspring. "Mama, would you listen to this child of yours—son, where did you hear this new-age philosophy," and he cocked his head askew; "have you been talking to those crazy new bears down in the valley, the ones who raid camps and eat out of—yuck!—garbage cans?"

"Son, humans aren't your friends, dear, even though some of them pretend to be; you don't remember your Aunt or Uncle, and that is because they too were fooled into thinking that humans were their friends, and they allowed ones like these before us to live amongst them, and when it was all over, the humans murdered them and took them and did something to them that is too terrible to mention, and then let your Aunt and Uncle stand upright in their human wooden structure in a way that makes them look alive—I know, darling, because the blue jay told me so, and he is not the kind of fellow that would lie about such a dreadful thing."

"So, they are just pretenders—like the time Cousin Bear's friend pretended to be my friend but he really wasn't."

"Exactly," Papa Bear said, and then fell back down to his meal.

Baby Bear then tore into the dead corpse with zest and fervor, and when he gulped a big chunk of meat and organ, he lifted his head up and cried, "It tastes just like chicken!"

The Bear Family laughed uproariously!

The townsfolk of this mountainous region got together and commissioned a professional sign maker to make them a fancy sign, and commissioned a professional writer to write them some fancy words; and after the citizens hemmed and hawed about it, and looked it up and down and sideways, and even from some angles most people would not even have thought of, they posted that hand-carved wooden sign right there and then on the very spot where those two intrepid interlopers into the wild had been consumed by their passions. And it still stands there today, if you want to travel the long trek up winding roads and into the rolling hills to behold its now clawed and scratched surface and read its still undisturbed message:

"For those of you who believe that wild animals are our not-so-distant relatives and are just a genetic tick away from being just like you and me and want to bond with them and be like them and put all of your trust in them and place your faith in them and put them before your fellow man, please go live with them somewhere else!"

-Finis-

Fat City

Crunch, snap, crackle, pop
Where is dat doggone fat gene at,
Slurp, gurgle, slobber, smack
Heck, look at dat dere soder pop!

Wendy the housewife was waddling down the waxen corridor of the local supplier of gas and super-caloric gastrointestinal delights. She, being a citizen of the free world in the richest country in the history of the human race, reasoned—but perhaps this is too strong a word for her; "decided" might be better suited for the simple machinery that inhabited her primitive skull—that as she was a free woman, and an independent woman who refused to starve herself to please any man, she had the immutable right to grab hold of as many brightly-colored, candy-coated chocolate bars as her chubby fingers could manage and then plop the insulin-spiking, sugar-filled, artery-clogging, saturated-fats-drenched, cancer-feeding, artificially-colored ticking time bombs—with a shortened molecular fuse—into her basket, which was already stuffed with other impossible-to-imagine-a-century-ago sweet treats and marbled animal flesh products. At the checkout counter, rows east and west and north and south of delectable fat and sugar concoctions sailed the message of "just a nibble" to the drooling, weak-willed patrons. There were three teens in front of her, two males and one female, each of whom carried a sixty-four-ounce supersized-supersaturated-sugar canteen drink in their pudgy hands, and each of whom carried about one hundred excess pounds of those now ubiquitous jiggling fat markers on their burgeoning forms.

"Mommy," a young girl asked her mother as she too waited in the long line on this cold day, "what is diabetes?"

"Well, Sarah, what a good question," the mother said, obviously proud and impressed, as evidenced by the quick nod of her own head and smile on her own face, "let's see—umm, it is when your pancreas—you know, it is in your body, here," and she pointed to where the blushing kidneys resided, "it makes insulin to help keep down your blood sugar, but when it gets too pooped to pop, it quits making insulin and your blood sugar rises and you can get real good and sick—like Uncle Jerry."

"What about juvenile diabetes?"

"Why, Sarah, how do you know about that?"

"My teacher taught us about it—he said we need to exercise and eat right to avoid diseases like that."

"Well, good for him," she said, stroking her daughter's silky, smooth, brown hair; "well, anyway, juvenile diabetes, well, umm, that is for juveniles—like yourself, I think…"

"Oh," Sarah said, contemplative, and then her unnaturally big arms—arms as big as a grown man's arms when he is physically fit—reached out to snatch, like a hungry wolf would for plump chickens, a handful of chocolate bars, and tossed them into the already-swelled-to-the-limit grocery basket. She smiled up at her adoring mother.

Her mother smiled and once more stroked her daughter's long, brown hair, and saw her pretty face, but her own eyes did not really transmit the proper image of the one hundred and eighty pounds of inordinate flesh that bulged out in the form of tragedy and betrayal, too much flesh crying foul and outrage that was tacked onto a too-young girl of just twelve years of age.

"Hello, Wendy," said the skinny clerk, "having a party?"

"No," she laughed, "just for snacks."

"Well, Sarah is a lucky girl to have a mother like that," he said, smiling.

"Hello," he said to the next customer.

"Hello," the slender adult female said, and plopped down a shiny can of Coke, six small white donuts, and a thick, chewy, nutty chocolate bar of rectangular shape and spectacular taste. "Breakfast," she announced, smiling.

"We are all just too busy these days to cook," the clerk said, dreaming of the wonderful financial rewards from the ridiculous amount of money his store made from selling such ridiculous foodstuffs for such ridiculous prices.

The three teens sucked the sweet colas as they jabbered and joked on their way to high school, and soon, they were in the locker rooms and slowly putting on their Physical Education uniforms and reluctantly reporting to Mr. Cool for instructions.

Mr. Cool, a middle-aged man and elite athlete, role model and passionate advocate for exercise and proper nutrition, actually not only demanded that his students engage in meaningful physical activity but also required that they learn why and how the activity was affecting their body in a positive manner. Today, he expected his students to participate in a four-hundred-and-forty-yard run, and the next day a mile run around the dirt track so he could complete the results for the Physical Education Standards as required by the State Department of Education.

"All right, you knuckleheads," he began, but he said it with affection, so no one was offended, "the first thing we have to do today is run a lap—are you listening, freshmen?—one lap! Now, I can't give you a grade if you don't even attempt the lap; so, when I call your name, come up to the starting line." He called ten names, and found one student missing. "Marilyn, Marilyn," he cried, looking round, "where are you—Marilyn?"

He found her standing off to the side with her friends. "Come on, Marilyn, it's time for your lap."

"I don't wanna," replied the girl.

"Look," he began, enthusiastically, "it's only a four-forty—four hundred and forty yards; it will only take a few minutes—you can even walk it if you feel you really can't run the entire thing, so, come on," he waved to her, but she just hunched her gigantic shoulders and frowned. Mr. Cool was exasperated, and walked over to the other Physical Education teacher, Mr. Baught. "Can you believe her, not even attempting to walk it!"

Mr. Baught looked toward the girl and shook his head. "Well, Jim, look at her, she must weigh over two hundred pounds—and look at my students over there," and he nodded behind him. "I have seven students who won't even suit up—and even after I told them they would at least get a 'C' if they just put on a pair of doggone shorts and came out to the track and attempted the course."

"Our time has come and gone," Jim said, looking at the mass of lazy students who were walking after running a mere one hundred yards down the track. His voice became dark, like the clamoring sound a coming augury of doom would make, had it sound and reason. "I read in the paper that the average high school lineman on a football team weighs more than the average professional football lineman of thirty years ago—now, Edward, that is just plain wrong, just plain wrong." He shook his head, and his voice became more somber. "What price will we pay when these lazy kids have children, and raise them the way they are being raised—but without even any small amount of the restraint and tiny amounts of common sense their parents still have?"

The three teens, after a disturbing period of having to exercise for a physically draining ten minutes before they whined and grumbled and quit, later went to their next class, each of them sure to gobble a candy bar on the way. At lunch, they went to the fast food death house off campus and purchased a gigantic hamburger, a huge bag of greasy fries and a large Coke that had a total of two thousand calories in them; the teens then went back to school and slept through their last remaining classes.

On their way home, they went back to the local convenience store and purchased more supersized drinks and then each of them proceeded home. Pantagruel, the smallest of the three friends, entered the doorway of his house at a very impressive two hundred and forty pounds of muscle, bone and blubber. Immediately he went to—and there was no doubt that he positively and absolutely went right to that magical instrument of destruction—that body destroyer, that mind slayer, that worthless pile of electronic circuits and hardened plastic: the video game, and commenced to put an enormous amount of time and energy into it. Three hours hence, and his mother walked in—tipping the scales at a more impressive two hundred and seventy pounds of soft muscle, thinning bone, and drooping blubber—and she sang hello to her boy and then went into the kitchen to hoist a small cake-like object into her gaping mouth. "Snack," she said, not once considering that she had just eaten more calories in this aggressive gulp than most fit people have during the course of a regular meal.

Soon, Papa Gargantua came home, and he, being the biggest of the threesome, tipped the scales at an absurdly impressive three hundred and twenty pounds of dwindling muscle, cracking bone and multitudinous layers of billowing blubber as he huffed and puffed through the doorway. "Home," he managed to utter as he wiped the heavy sweat off his thick brows, for the walk from the car had tired him out.

"I don't know what to do about dinner, honey," Mama Gargantua said, after kissing her man; "it's been so hectic at the office, I'm too tired to even think about cooking."

"Let's go out," he said, and then, turning his head toward the family room wherein dwelt Son Gargantua, "Let's go, Pantagruel, we're going out to eat!"

"Awesome," Pantagruel shouted.

The restaurant was packed, as it always was, and every citizen who could manufacture a ready excuse not to cook at home was there or at some other restaurant, scarfing mounds of greasy, sugary food down their moist gullet, just as if it was a conveyor belt leading to the stinking sewer. Alas, this was not the primordial forest of our ancestors where the humans labored all the day long and then ate their well-deserved food that came from the good, green earth; no, this was the prime rib forest, where humans of diverse shapes—but mostly of balloon shape—with massive arms pumped up like big balloons and massive thighs like bursting-to-pop balloons and bigger-than-the-biggest-pumpkin-ever-grown bellies that seemed to be still growing balloons and enormous buttocks like the crazy-circus-clown buttocks; and people here, had they lived one hundred years ago, would certainly have had employment as the circus freak fat-man and circus freak fat-lady; and there was every kind of lopsided, clothes-bursting, belt-busting, button-popping, eye-rubbing, and I-can't-believe-I-just-saw-something-human-that-big shape, and soon it became the most grotesque forest of all, with misshapen bodies and limbs of all kinds, and misshapen bodies of all ages, and misshapen bodies of all genders, creeds, and races—overindulgence in foodstuff is an equal opportunity supplier of destroying human health—and useless, hideous, bizarre folds of doughy blubber; and in this forest of degenerate and, more importantly, shameless eating that had no parallel in human history, a bizarre landscape of humans crunching and gnawing and slurping not for survival but simply for pleasure and gorging reigned—where no intellectual audience from history past would comprehend the perversion therein; and, if this was not enough, if one were to add up the entire caloric content of the food shoveled—just like a crane operator shovels—and sucked—just like a pack of hyenas suck the blood and guts out of a kill—and swallowed whole—just like a snake swallows a mouse—in one day here, why, that food could fairly feed an entire poor village of three hundred people in a remote country for an entire month and allow them to experience some kind of health.

"Pantagruel," Papa Gargantua said, "how are your studies going this year?"

"Okay, I guess; I just don't have the time to study."

"I know what you mean, son," he returned, "those Teachers give out too much homework; well, you just do the best you can, eh, champ?" and he playfully winked at his boy.

"I saw Dr. Morton this morning," Mama Gargantua began, "and asked him if he had recommendations for me to lose some weight; I asked him about bypass surgery, or information about the latest weight-loss programs, and you know what he said?" but her husband could not respond—he had to finish chewing on a mouthful of rare steak and heavily buttered potato and thick, oily gravy—so she had the go-ahead to continue. "He said that weight-loss programs don't work, and that you are only losing water weight and muscle—can you believe that malarkey? So, I asked him about a pill or something, some kind of pill I could take to help me lose weight, you know, like the kind that absorbs carbohydrates, and wouldn't you know what he said?" But her husband was now masticating another enormous helping of food in his mouth, so once again, she continued. "He said that we shouldn't eat just anything that is put before us that tastes good—is he crazy? Are we supposed to eat boring junk all day, like those health-nut wackos who eat bird seed and stuff that tastes like cardboard all the time and are so skinny? And then he had the nerve to say, 'and how about the magic pill called exercise?' Well, sir, I was so mortified, it was a miracle I did not just walk right out of there and go complain to the insurance company—why, we pay good money to go to the doctor, and all we get is grief. What good are doctors if they aren't there to help us? And who has time for exercise these days—it's a different world we live in—just rush, rush, rush!" And immediately following this passionate outburst, she proceeded to just gobble, gobble, gobble her heaping helping of foodstuff that had enough calories in it to feed a physically fit man for an entire day.

Papa Gargantua, his mouth momentarily halted from its incessant gobbling mechanism, said, with righteous indignation, "Outrageous, just outrageous—it's prejudice against people who are a tad bit overweight, that's what it is," and in a moment he was shoveling food in a way that exceeded the expertise of a forklift operator.

The Gargantuas went home and Papa went to his small office to work on his projects and Mama went to the phone to work on her projects, and the Son went back to the video games, and was later joined by Papa; later that night, they came together to watch family movies and family television shows and eat some richly layered buttered and heavily salted popcorn and a few sandwiches, and then soon it was bedtime.

In the morning, they arose and skipped breakfast here, knowing they would have breakfast at any place they fancied. Papa and Mama Gargantua drove away, and as Son Gargantua walked down the street, checking to see if he had enough money to buy food at the local in-with-health-and-out-with-disease fast food store that always, always, always had a long line of the just-too-busy-to-cook-breakfast crowd, he passed 1067 Bluebird Drive, never once looking at the two people who had just parked in the driveway there.

The two people, a man and woman, walked into the house and hugged the woman who lived there. "How is John?" the man asked.

His sister said, "The same."

The wife of the man said, "Did he sleep well?"

"Yes, I suppose so," the woman said.

"Breakfast," the man said, after entering the house and greeting John.

The countenance of John lit up. "Yeah," he said, with great difficulty, "how was the trip?"

"Good, I guess," the man said, "but we're home now."

Throughout the day, the three people worked on projects related to their jobs, visited with John, gave food to him, helped him with his hygienic needs, and played with him. It was a typical day in the life of this home.

A knock came at the door. The husband had invited a friend over—despite the protestations of the women—to conference with them about John. Jim Cool walked into the room wherein John lay on his super-supported, multilayered, steel-reinforced bed; the blood drained from Jim's face and his heart beat loudly and he felt tears welling up in his eyes—but he was a man, and being a man, he restrained the tears and smiled as he shook the hand of the youth. He spent the day with the family and at night sat down with them and issued words that were neither friendly nor polite.

"Do you people know what you're doing to him?" he said, finally allowing his indignation to burst forth. "For goodness' sake, Pete," he shouted, looking at his friend, "I added up the calories you are giving him a day—do you know how many calories," and he looked to the now-fuming women, too, "you are force-feeding him? You heard me—force-feeding him!"

"No," the sister said, angrily, but being polite, she would say nothing more.

But her sister-in-law was not as mannerly as she. "Look, Jim, I know Pete asked you here to consult about John, but you are an outsider; you just can't come in here and judge us without knowing the complete history of John, and all the things we have done for him; we love him and would never do anything to deliberately hurt him."

"Oh, really, is that so?" Jim returned, shaking his head, his voice full of exasperation and vexation, and now his voice went up a few decibels as he stood up. "Do you know that you are feeding him nearly nine thousand calories a day; every day, that is what you are feeding him—nine thousand calories—so don't tell me you have his best interests at heart; for goodness' sake, people, John is only twenty-seven, and he already has a death sentence hanging over him."

"Pete, are you going to let him talk that way to me?" the wife shouted.

Pete, with a cool demeanor, looked to Jim and then to his wife, and his words were not full of wild emotion, as he had already worked out this confrontational scenario. "Sit down, Amy, and listen to the man." He turned away from her and looked to his friend. "Please, continue."

"Thank you," Jim said, nodding, and then, looking to the wife, "look, Amy, it's nothing personal, it's just I don't like what is happening to John, and I do care, believe me, I do, that's what I do for a living, and it's the way I live—helping people who want my help—but I will leave right now if you want me to." He felt calmer and thus said, "Look, I apologize if I was rude to you, but it's just that I want everyone to have the chance to be healthy and happy, and right now, John doesn't have that chance."

The two antagonists embraced, and the session continued.

Jim looked at his paperwork and massaged his face and then looked up at the silent trio. "John weighs nine hundred pounds." Yes, the trio knew this, but hearing it from another person, an expert in the field of nutrition and exercise, helped them see the incredible impact of this statement in stark, revelatory language.

Jim recommended that tests be done to determine what diseases John had and other tests to determine the amount of damage inflicted upon his body by the massive weight; but in the meantime, he laid out a carefully constructed plan regarding proper caloric intake, the proper amount of carbohydrates, fats and protein, and vitamins and minerals needed, and the right kind of exercise that would bring John back from his prostrate prison. The brother and sister and sister-in-law were in agreement. The great experiment began that moment.

Sometime later, actually a great amount of time later, after John was eating a normal amount of food and after doctors

Ray Dacolias

had tested him for diseases and other disorders, and after John began to perform the briefest and easiest exercises available, he was standing on the local high school track in the middle of the night. His family stood next to him.

"Jim," he said nervously, looking at his mentor, "how long will it be—I mean, how long will it take me—until I'm normal again?"

Jim smiled, and walked up to his finest pupil and placed his hand on the man's massive shoulders. "John, it all starts with that first important movement forward, when you know you will never go back…" He nodded his head and walked away.

The great hulking body of John trembled as he stared at the dirt track. "I have to earn every bit of food I eat," he said, "I know this now; O, I do want this, I do want to be normal—it's been so long since I could just do what I did as a kid, that I have forgotten what it was like—but this time, this time…" He swallowed and breathed in slowly and exhaled out slowly and then cautiously and carefully lifted his giant right leg up and out and down on the track and then did the same with his left leg and then moved his huge arms forward and began to walk. "One small step for a man…"

-Finis-

Steel Maiden

The following story was told to me thirty years ago by Admiral John L. Garfield. He died in 2003, the last known witness to the remarkable events surrounding the finding of the Steel Maiden. I promised him that I would not divulge the contents of his tale until the Navy declassified certain documents pertaining to the famous ship. As I write, these documents are being published in the *New York Times*, *Wall Street Journal* and *Washington Post*, and you may read them with great interest and still wonder if the entire affair actually happened, but I am here to tell you that it did, and I will now supply the proof that will make you believe it.

When I was a much younger man, I lived in a small apartment complex that was directly across the street from a state university. During the day, I would work, and during the night, I attended classes there. I was always in a hurry, often coming home from my labors and gathering up my books and dashing across the street and over the sprawling green lawn of the campus and running up the stone steps in front of the tall school building and falling into my seat just as the professor began his lecture.

There was a cluster of apartments that sat on the other side of the street, but I had no occasion to inspect them, for they meant nothing to me. One day, when I was walking back from a class that had ended early and actually allowed me to observe the parting of day and the coming of night, I happened to look up to one of the two-story apartments and therein I saw a man sitting on a balcony with oxygen tubes fitted into his nostrils. I don't know why I did it—maybe because I was young and healthy and just for a brief moment I felt a kinship with someone I knew had once been young and healthy like me—but I waved at him.

He waved back at me, and a faint smile appeared on his wrinkled face. I became embarrassed and coerced a smile and then continued on toward my home. By that night I had forgotten all about that innocent wave, but its symbolic gesture would not forget me.

Weeks later, I was walking down the long, concrete sidewalk toward my apartment, when I happened to look up and I once more beheld the man standing there with the oxygen tubes and green tank. I felt lousy that I had forgotten all about this man, and once again I waved, and once again he waved back, smiling.

This time, when I walked into my apartment, I began to think about that old man living up in that apartment, perhaps alone, perhaps lonely, perhaps having no one in his life or any good thing to look forward to except a wave or smile from a passerby. I felt horrible, and I wanted to go back and find the man and talk to him, but I reasoned that my studies took precedence and so I abandoned the thought of the man and fell into doing what was easy and uncomplicated—studying; yes, to study meant I did not have to risk communicating with a human being who might present certain complications in my life, such as wanting to talk to me longer than a few minutes and thus interfere with my complicated schedule, but the more I sought to justify my impersonal attitude I inflicted on this man, the more it became clear that I was wrong in my assumptions.

The next day I looked for him, but he was not there, nor the next day, nor the next month, and presently I decided that he had either moved or been taken ill. I had missed my chance to experience brotherhood and bring joy to a person who may have needed just a precious few minutes a day to feel alive and happy. But I was young, and being callous is easy when you have all the wealth in the world you need and no hindrances before you.

Months passed by, and I no longer looked up at the spot where the man had once sat. Then one day, as I was leisurely walking back home after an exhilarating course on WWII, for some reason still unknown to me, I happened to gaze up and there he was again. He waved and I waved, but this time I would not miss my chance. I moved closer until I stood nearly under the balcony and shouted, "Hello!"

He took out the oxygen tubes and whispered in a barely audible voice, "Hello, youngster," and then, putting the white tubes back into his nostrils, he managed a small smile.

I now knew that if I did not say something further, I would fail myself as a man, and so I said, "May I come up?"

He responded as men often do, with a backward nod of his head to indicate approval, and so I ascended the steps and soon I was before his pale white door, which I soon knocked upon. I was nervous and afraid because I was out of my protective, artificial element, but instinctively knew that this was the right thing to do because one day we all get old and somehow I knew it was my duty to visit the elderly and those ill and bring comfort to them. I heard his slow shuffling of shoes across the carpet and then the door opened slowly to reveal a tall, slender gentleman. He smiled and extended his hand, and said in a quiet voice, "Come in, young man." I shook his weak hand and walked through the doorway. He closed the door and pointed toward a small beige sofa. I sat down upon it and he sat down upon a small grey sofa across from me. He smiled warmly again, a smile that told me visitors rarely came here and that he was pleased to have company. "I am John Garfield," he stated, and then I told him my name. I remember thinking that this was just some old man sitting in front of me, that he had lived his life and now his life was nearly over, just another simple man who had lived a simple life and needed a little conversation; I remember thinking that he was not unlike all other older people I had seen around town, just ordinary folk who had lived ordinary lives and who now lived in an ordinary town, for if they had not lived ordinary lives, then why were they here and not in some special place with all of the other special people? Yet, as I was to learn, and I am very glad to have learned this early in life, you never know who you are sitting across from, regardless of their age or gender or present station in society.

We engaged in polite conversation, as all people do when they first meet, and presently he offered me a glass of water and a small cracker, which I politely accepted. He was curious about my studies, and I was glad to elaborate on my classes, as talking about things that I intimately know puts me at ease.

But I must tell you about his speech. It was halting and sporadic, and quite often he could not talk for long periods of time because of the problem of his lungs. This first visit did not last long because he was in great pain, and soon I was at the door and promising to return. When I shook his hand again,

I noticed how strong it was this time, and then I turned and walked down the stairs and out into the cool night air and regained the well-trodden route to my apartment, wherein I would once more resume my frenetic life.

Three months later, spring break arrived and my classes were over. I had been to see John on many occasions, but I could never stay too long, either because of my studies or because of his illness; but now, I could visit him in the morning when he could breathe better and I could stay longer. So, one very hot and humid day, I walked up the stairs to his apartment and knocked on the door and in a moment I was sitting comfortably on the beige sofa. He was comfortable too, having long ago accepted me as someone who could talk to him about intel-lectual and cultural issues he cared passionately about, and I had accepted him as someone who could talk about current events I cared deeply about.

He was sitting there with the green tank and a glass of lemonade next to him on the small dresser, when he took out the tubes and visited upon me a visage born of pathos and passion, a look I had not yet seen in him, a look that signaled he was now turning over those long-ago remnants of his life that many of us bury as we grow older.

"I have no family," he said, in his guttural whisper; "the Navy was my life; oh, I was married once, but that was so very long ago." He lifted up his head and his now predominantly misty emerald-colored eyes looked around, but then he nod-ded the agony away. "A man does not want to die with secrets that should be shared with the world, it is never a good thing, he needs someone to pass them on to; I have waited a long time for that someone—someone who reminds me of who I once was and the friends I once had and the way we were together; you are like my friends of old, you would have been my friend when I was young." He had gone too long without the precious oxygen and so he hooked up the clear tubes and inhaled deeply for a while and then, when he felt able, he withdrew them and let them dangle again. "I hate these tubes, I really do, but I earned them, too, I did, so I guess if I had to do everything all over again I would do everything the same and still be sitting with these troublesome tubes; but now I can tell you about it all, and that is worth it all, as long as someone else knows—but that will be the hard part, to break the silence to someone, to break the vow I took, to keep quiet about a mission I was proud to be attached to and a Navy I loved; but I have to tell someone, now, before it is too late."

I was growing nervous now, as if he were going to tell me about war atrocities or other moral dilemmas that would burden my conscience, but I could do nothing but simply sit there and listen because of the time I had spent with him—I had given too much of myself to him and received too much of him over too long a period to leave now. He took more oxygen.

The environs of the room seemed to change when he began again, and as I remember it, it was precisely that the room grew very dark and very quiet, as if something mystical had entered unseen and unheard by me.

"It was 1944 and the war was not yet won—but of course you, being a good reader of history, know that—and the Allies would prosecute war to the end but they were more afraid that the axis powers would gain one weapon we feared the most: the atomic bomb." I grew numb when I heard this, but the thrill of hearing wartime espionage grew inside me with a fury. "There are many things the public never hears that it should never hear about, secrets they have no business hearing, even with declassified documents, because some documents will never be declassified and some will never be seen again

by anyone—and shouldn't be, either." He took another generous helping of sweet oxygen. He leaned over and whispered,
"Everyone thinks the first atomic testing was in 1945 in New
Mexico, but I am here to tell you it was a year earlier, because
I was part of the team that was dispatched to retrieve the real
first bomb that was sunk as it was being transported across
the North Atlantic to be dropped on Germany."

I nearly fainted. Was it possible he was simply an old man
with dementia, I thought; had he been fooling me all these long
months, only now to reveal his true madness to me? What was
I to do, agree with him about something I knew was histori-
cally inaccurate and impossible to conceal from the public for
so long? But what could I now do but simply sit and listen, it
was the courteous thing to do, and then maybe I would walk
through those familiar doors and down those familiar steps,
never to return again; after all, he had no hold over me, we
had exchanged no gifts, we were not engaged in any common
project; I would abrogate the time we had spent together in a
moment to preserve my own uncomplicated and smooth life.
I watched him gain more precious oxygen and then he continued on. I was incredulous to the utmost.

"I know at this point in my narration you think me a very
confused old man, youngster, but give me time, and you will
believe." I decided then that he was either very, very sane or
very, very mad. "The *U.S.S. Lincoln* had been carrying the bomb
when it was sunk by a German sub, and it was the worry of
the military brass and Roosevelt that the Germans had targeted the ship because they knew the bomb was on it, and
that they would try to retrieve it; we knew the Germans had
been working on the bomb, but we did not know how far they
had gotten into the process, but that wouldn't matter if they
got hold of it, so my unit and others shipped out to the site

where the ship had sunk. We were Navy frogmen, the best."
He took a long, luxurious draught of the magic elixir as he sat
with a serene look upon his wrinkled countenance, as if a great
responsibility had been lifted from him, as if, finally, he was
being freed, slowly and surely, from the chains and bonds of
harder times. "We arrived at a point about a few hundred miles
south of Newfoundland, in waters that were more than twelve
thousand feet deep; and although I was eager and pleased to
be part of this operation, I was worried that we were wast-
ing our time. I went to our C.O. and asked him why we were
going to dive in frigid waters—summer though it was—and
in waters too deep to search. I will never forget what he said;
it has served me well all these years. 'Lieutenant, there are
more fantastic things in this world than you or I should ever
know.' In a moment I knew he was right, for soon I beheld
the X-1, the first deep-research vehicle of its kind—a miniature submarine that could withstand great depths like its
papa subs and could take two men inside it; technology that
would not be available to the commercial world for ten more
years. War," he said, closing his eyes, "the mother of inven-
tion—what we will do to win and kill each other swifter and
with more efficiency…"

I wondered what he was seeing now by blocking out the
stimulus of my world and seeing the indwelt horrors that had
been sutured inside his—in this case, the lurching, jagged
crush of memories being the fine fibers that bind—into his
restless brain by the horrors of war—in this case, the sanguinary long of it and the slaughtering short of it and the
unbound murdering depth of it and the magnified wicked-
ness of it all; how tragic for those, I pondered, who could
neither escape the hurtful past by eyes open or shut. I later
understood that the terrible price we pay for the defense

and preservation of freedom can never be understood by the unaffected and undetached.

He took another long draught of oxygen and then continued, as if his mind was anxious to spill out the contents of its history right now and in one unbroken sequence. "I queried the C.O. about the sub and its usefulness in such waters, and he was quick to inform me that there was a geological map of the sea bottom that had been as of late drawn with sonar and that indicated a small cluster of mountain regions at about two thousand feet in depth that might support even a massive destroyer, and that if this were not so, the mission would be over quickly enough, as speed was tantamount to avoid enemy detection here.

"Still, two men from our squadron took a quick dive and reported no immediate presence of the sunken ship. I was senior in rank, and so I went into one of the subs with the driver, and another of our squadron went into the other sub with his driver, and soon we were lowered into the icy waters and we were on our way." As he felt the tingling of exhaustion moving over him, he realized the folly of speaking too quickly, so he took a long course of the liquid gold until he felt strong enough to speak again. His face took on a strangely youthful glow of wonder and excitement, the same expression small children reveal when they listen to a story about that most mythical of creatures, Santa Claus. His voice was filled with enthrallment as he closed his eyes and let his head rest against the soft, brown leather of the rocker. "So strange it all was as we peered through the small window; so dark, so unbelievably pitch black, so—still, so eerily silent, that I—a creature of incessant fury and noise—felt a growing peacefulness in my heart that I had never known." A gentle smile lit up his pale countenance. "And as our small light shone on creatures and landscapes that no human being had ever seen, I felt privileged, and honored; yes, humbled even, to see such a regal world that had been hidden from us—an entire universe not yet destroyed by Man; and I remember hoping my ambitious Brothers and Sisters would never come down here and ruin this indigenous population…like they had done in their own dominion, so many times before." He paused for a moment as he shook his head, his countenance full of a profound sorrow. He soon pressed on. "We soon came upon the weird landscape below—long rows of mountain ridges just like ours above—and we grew excited when we sighted the design of a ship, but we did not radio it in, because it might have been the wreck of any ship, so we waited, and waited, and kept diving deeper and listening to the soft purring motor of this sub as it swam closer and closer and closer until we soon realized that it was not our destroyer; no, not our ship, no, not the *Lincoln*, it was another, another from a long time ago and from a fantasy world far, far away…" His voice stopped and I thought he would again slip the tubes in, but he did not. His voice was nearly hysterical. "It was not our ship—it was the Steel Maiden. You call it the *Titanic*."

I was altered in every sense and thought. What was I to do now—disown what he had just said? Everything thus far spoken by his lips had seemed plausible, not at all given to hyperbole or fabrication. I tried to grasp reality but when he continued on with his story, reality took a holiday from my reeling mind.

Now, he took a great gorging of oxygen and let it flow and settle into his damaged body like a gulp of warm sunshine. His demeanor calmed as his head fell back and his eyes shut and he allowed the powerful blasts of the revitalizing liquid to pour into his every vessel and capillary, where they unloaded their liberating cargo to every anxious cell; he did not speak for several minutes as he sat motionless and allowed his ravaged body to repossess a semblance of sensibility. I moved nary a muscle and urged my mind to analyze the information recently unfurled before me. It did not matter now what I thought about this weird tale, for now I was a willful prisoner caught in the steely web of curiosity.

His breath was slower now and measured now and when he opened his eyes, he had not opened them to see my world but the world he had once explored under the surface of the sea on that summer night in 1944; I do not believe that he even saw me there when he again began to speak of the ship that had become such a great myth that seemed better not to be found, a story that should never be completed, so that its epic disaster could sustain our interests for all time. No one wants to see the rubble of empires wherein great men and women once walked.

"We came upon the great heap of steel that had broken into two large pieces—only one piece sitting before us—and neither of us spoke," he said, slowly, his face ablaze with wonder; "we knew it was the *Titanic* because of the sheer size of it, the magnificent shape of it, the place where it lay; we knew it must be it, and as we came closer and saw its name still scrawled across its sides, still, I felt a chill sweep across my body—the *Titanic*, after so long, resurrected in my consciousness, lying there in her sublime beauty for my eyes only. I did not radio in because I did not want to share even the thought of her with anyone." He paused and I thought he would take a break, but he did not. "The driver took the sub closer and soon we were hovering right next to her bulk, skimming along and admiring the workmanship of the vessel but also looking for that long gash from the iceberg that had taken her down on her maiden voyage. We never found that hole."

Now, he had eclipsed his allotted time without his constant companion, oxygen, and so took the tubes with his slender hands and in one continuous motion slipped them into his nostrils and inhaled deeply many times and then took them out and once more spoke.

"We still had not radioed in, and in my mind I had no intention to do so presently, and neither did I speak of this reluctance to the driver, for I felt that both of us did not want to share this grand moment of discovery—we were part of history, now, co-founders of a great find—and suddenly the war seemed far away and irrelevant, as if the machinations of man had slipped into their own abyss as the image of the fallen Lady before us ascended into our theater of the sublime. We were moving around the hull of the ship when I nearly fainted. I heard a sound emanating from outside our sub, and the driver halted our progression as we lingered near the hull." He leaned over, and though he was facing me and seeming to look at me, I still do not think he saw me; he was seeing his Steel Lady. His voice was a low whisper now, frightened and urgent. "It was a tap, tap, tapping sound—tap, tap, tap—like Morse code—and I was shaking and sweating and the driver was sweating and shaking as we frantically began looking about for something to seize us out of our nightmare when…" But his oxygen had run low, so he once more grabbed the tubes and soon the job was done, and he resumed his narrative, his voice still filled with urgency.

"We were looking and looking and looking to find something to assuage our insane thoughts when we happily and joyfully saw through the small, glass porthole a long, steel cable that was banging against the side of the ship—tap, tap, tap—and then we both laughed, O, how we laughed so hard and so gratefully long; we were so relieved and we looked at each other and laughed again and then finally the laughter died away and we went back to inspecting the hull, and then the tap, tap, tapping noise began again, but when we looked to the steel cable, it was no longer moving in the currents; no, there was another sound, and now we sat perfectly still and listened, but not afraid this time, for we knew that there had to be some logical explanation to this other sound, but then the tapping sound began to transform into our mind—into letters—yes, into letters; we had been trained in Morse code, and whenever I heard a collection of sounds strung together, I instinctively heard them as codes; and now I heard letters, impossible letters strung together that were coming from a ship that had been downed thirty-two years ago but seemingly thirty-two centuries ago—other countries had their ancient myths and this was ours, so why not assign it to a very long time ago so that its physical presence might not be captured again? The sweat was pouring off me because I knew those letters—I did—I knew what those letters meant…"

He was exhausted again, and in need of his liquid medicine, and so he took another long inhale of the gaseous stuff and once more laid his head of white hair against the rocker and closed his eyes to rest. He seemed to rest for a long time, and I even thought he had fallen asleep, when, after several minutes, he leaned forward, now cobalt-blue eyes blazing—yes, he had multi-colored irises—and when I looked into them, it was like looking into the very soul of the sunlit sea—and his voice was punctuated with passion. "The sound," he began again, still in that ardent whisper, as if he had not missed a second of speaking, "that tap, tap, tapping code—it was as familiar to me as the sound of birds singing above: S.O.S.!"

My face blanched shock and awe.

I had heard this much and this much I knew, he was no madman, no victim of senility, no fraudulent disciple of the past, but what he had just said melted my sense of fairness toward him and I began to look askew at this old man, as if he were hiding something from me—as if he had been hiding something from me all these past months that I, in my naïve youth, had missed.

Still, he pressed on, unbowed. "It obviously was an S.O.S., but I knew it had to be another loose steel cable or some such natural phenomenon, and as the pilot swung the sub around to look for the origins of this noise, we found none, none ostensibly, so in my mind—I never spoke of it to the pilot— it was an internal object ceaselessly battering itself against the steel armor, and I was going to leave it at that when I, for reasons I will never understand, bent down and took the lever that manipulated the mechanical arm outside the sub and aimed it at the hull and banged it slowly—S.O.S.—a few times and then stopped. I guess I had to do it, and the pilot, I think, knew I had to, too, even though we both knew the whole episode was absurd, but we had to reassure ourselves that it was so, so years later we would not have to even for a moment think about it. Nothing came, nothing came back at all—of course, nothing came back, and I let my erect posture sag and I breathed a sigh of relief and let down the mechanical arm and then watched as the pilot began the motor, and then we heard it, the sound of taps which issued a message that crushed us worse than any ocean depths—HELP!" He paused. "The messenger was alive!"

I watched the absolute horror of it all manifest itself on his aged face, and I can tell you now that this was no dream he was reliving, no hallucination he was seeing, no tall tale he was telling; it was something he truly believed in.

I decided to no longer analyze everything I was hearing and simply listen. He took more oxygen.

"I immediately tapped back the following message, 'who are you?', while expecting nothing back because nothing could have tapped it back, don't you see? It was impossible; and I did it, I defend my actions by saying I had to do it to show myself that it was not at all supernatural but natural, and then we waited, but not long, no," his voice lowered, as if into a mystical place, "for the new message said, 'we…are…alive'!" He was almost weeping now, his lips palpitating, his eyes knit in frustration as he continued. "I tapped back—automatically, for now I was merely a radioman on the other end of a message—that we were U.S. Navy personnel on a mission, and I asked them to identify themselves. The message came back. 'We are survivors.' But then suddenly I just burst out laughing and turned to the pilot, who too burst out laughing. We had both been duped! It had been the men in the other sub playing tricks on us, I shouted, and he quickly and gratefully agreed with me. I radioed in to the crew up top and they told us the other sub had mechanical trouble and was presently on board, and they wanted to know what we had found; but since I could no longer think coherently nor speak eloquently, they were not to receive a reply. I had just made the greatest discovery in the world and was not about to share it with anyone else but the pilot." He took a great gulp of oxygen and went on speaking. "I then began an exchange of words with whoever—or whatever—was on the other side, and it told us some of the people had survived when the ship went down and fell upon this mountain ridge, and that somehow, they had landed in a section that had air pockets breathing out oxygen constantly—I had heard about such things; air pockets under the water that had sustained divers when they were desperate for oxygen. I asked them, incredulous though I was, how they had survived otherwise, and they replied—I supposed it was 'they' because sometimes there was a delay in the response, as if whoever was tapping was conferring with another—and they said that they had used nets found on board and made hooks from various utensils on board to thrust out through sunken windows in the bottom of the ship to catch fish daily, and to haul in seaweed and mollusks and all kinds of sea life for nourishment. I asked them how they had survived without sunlight. They quickly responded that their health was indeed poor and that some had already gone blind while others were nearly blind, but that, somehow, consuming so much varied seafood had sustained them. They also said that early on, some of the braver of the men had tried to leave the ship and swim to the top, but these men never returned. Of course, they wanted to be rescued, but to that I did not respond directly, for I knew what the real answer would be once I went to the C.O. and explained to him what we had found—if he would even believe us—so I told them that we would get back to them as soon as we could. I cannot remember any other time in my life when I did not want to break off a conversation with someone—there was so much I wanted to know from them."

He grabbed the tubes and this time shoved them into his nostrils as if they were now acknowledged as an irritant to him. His handsome visage was drawn in grave lines now.

"We had to continue our mission, but we could not think of anything other than what we had just heard; and yes, we did find the sunken *U.S.S. Lincoln*, and it had fallen not too far from our Lady, but it now lay upside down and so it would be very difficult to get inside her; so, our job being done, we resurfaced and soon found ourselves debriefing with the C.O.. He was not a man of great imagination."

He closed his eyes again and a profound sorrow contaminated his gentle visage. "I told him what we had heard and he immediately dismissed it as hallucination due to our experiencing extreme pressures at such depths, and that science would substantiate his claim; but I would not alter my report and the C.O. would not alter his stance, and there we were, two men of granite who would not yield to what they saw as a weaker version of themselves, and then he said, 'Officer, it does not matter what you found down there—for all I care, you could find Atlantis or mermaids or the Olympians perched on Mt. Olympus—and I wouldn't care one whit unless what you found could help us either retrieve that sunken bomb or win this blasted war; these are my orders, soldier, to see if the *Lincoln* is here and if so, get the bomb back, and if not, then get out of here as quickly as possible'; so now, he said, it was our job to try and retrieve the bomb and if not, then get out of there as swiftly as possible and hope and pray that the enemy did not know what was up and did not have the technology to bring the bomb up themselves. He turned and walked away and ordered two other men into the sub and two other men into the now-repaired sub and to immediately put the subs into the water. The C.O. ordered the pilot and myself confined to our quarters for the duration of the mission. I was a prisoner now of my own doing."

He took more oxygen.

"When our ship was moving, I had no knowledge of what had happened, except that we were leaving quickly enough to make me believe that our attempt to retrieve the bomb had failed. We pulled into the harbor at New York and the C.O. came to my cabin and stood before me like my father used to when he was about to verbally scourge me. 'Lieutenant,' he said, 'what you just saw and did in the Atlantic will remain classified for the duration of your natural life or until such time as the government sees fit to release documents pertaining to the events there,' and he threw down a piece of paper for me to read and sign, which stated what he had said, 'and from this moment on, any such mention of those events will be taken as treason,' he finished, grim faced, and then turned and left. Later, I saw the pilot but made no contact with him, and I spent the remainder of the war at a naval academy. I was now constantly watched."

He shook his head and frowned. "I, who had given my life's blood to the Navy, was now considered a security risk, a man to be followed—my phone was tapped, my letters opened and read, my friends and family questioned and detained; but when the war was over, all of this paranoia was over. I was free." He took more oxygen. "I was free but I was not free, for every day I thought of the sunken Lady and the incredible story of the survivors, and I wanted to believe that our government would have, after the war's end, immediately gone down there to the ship and tried to rescue those poor, courageous people. But I knew the way secret documents are treated, even ones that do not have to be secret any longer, how the government—I mean, any government—sometimes covers up things for no apparent reason except that they feel they must cover them up, if only because they can; the war was over and that was that—but now we were worried that the Communists might get the bomb, so I knew the documents would still be suppressed. But the Communists got the bomb anyway and other countries got it and I wondered when, when would we do the right thing and go down there and try and help those poor people? I soon realized that the entire mission had probably been forgotten and now nobody either cared about it or thought the whole affair to be a fabrication—except me, and the pilot; so, one day I looked up the pilot and I found him to be as consumed with the entire affair of the sunken Lady as was I—dreaming about it and thinking about it and wondering about it—and so, we two, once we thought it was safe, and once the military technology of the mini-subs was available to the public, rented a ship and took a small sub and headed off toward Newfoundland in the summer of 1967." He took a long swig of oxygen and then breathed heavily in and then heavily out and then took another swig of juicy oxygen and let it swirl around in his banged-up lungs until he felt the gingerly wallop of the small molecules bathing his cells in their sweet pulp. Now—now he looked at me with full cognizance of who I was as he continued his story. "We anchored near the spot where we had been twelve years previous and used sonar to find the ship, and when we did, we engaged the mini-sub and took off down into the dark waters, not even speculating on what we might find. Soon, we were there, and incredibly enough, it was there too, the *Titanic*, still precariously perched on that mountain ridge; but after a short journey, we did not find the *U.S.S. Lincoln*. It had either fallen or been knocked off its rocky ledge or had been retrieved by—someone."

He paused and his face became grave and his words became melancholy. "We found the Lady and found the same spot where once so long ago we had communicated to them inside her, and we commenced the tapping of Morse code, but nothing came; and we tapped and tapped and tapped for the longest time, and then went round her and tapped at various points of her hull but we could not get a message back. We resurfaced and came down again several times, refusing to give up, refusing to believe that the world had abandoned these miraculous people to a certain death, refusing to believe that we had imagined it all so long ago; now, the last time we went down we went right to the original spot of the tapping but this time we saw something through the thick debris that we had not seen before—markings on the side of the ship, weird, seemingly aimless squiggles and curving lines and loops that almost looked like hieroglyphics that were buried in soot and dust."

He took a quick gulp of oxygen—not too long at all this time, but obviously sufficient enough to keep him going. He leaned over and drew the markings that had been in his mind all these long years.

{ ⟩ ⟩ ⊐ | _ = ( ) _ ⌣

"We then took the mechanical arm and used it to push away the caked mud and debris from the letters, and slowly we saw letters form right before us." He leaned over and began to connect the strange shapes, still speaking in that low, desperate whisper. "We did not know what to expect: were they letters from a foreign country, from our country, from—whom?"

I looked in astonishment as the words began to appear on the sheet of white paper before me.

{} ⊢? | ∟ ⊏ (⟩ |

He was nearly done and I screwed up my eyes and looked at the words with bewilderment, for my mind was expecting one thing but the message before me was delivering another; and then, right there before me, the answer appeared.

A P R I L F O O L

I suddenly looked up, my thoughts still muddied, but I saw no one, no man before me, no rocking chair, nothing but the blank, boring white walls of my apartment. I screamed and stood up and looked around the room, my chest heaving and my breath fast as I searched about the place in my confusion, and then in my confusion I opened the door and jumped down the cement stairs and ran across the street and to the apartment complex near the college and I looked up at a certain balcony and there I saw an elderly gentlemen who had tubes that were attached to a green oxygen tank and that were going into his nostrils. I instinctively waved at him and he waved back and then I said hello, and he took out the tubes and said hello, to which I responded, may I come up, to which, after returning the tubes to his nostrils, and like so many men round the world, he nodded backward with his head that this was acceptable.

I stood there for a moment and then tore up those steps and knocked on the door and in an instant I was inside his small apartment. His name was John Garfield, and he had retired from the Navy and was simply enjoying what little life there was left to him.

-Finis-

The Epiphany of Pain

His body had always been the captain of his ship, steering him along one well-established and fairly simple course. There had never been any reason for him to disobey or dissuade these prescient commands, for he had always led with his fleshly desires, and anything that satiated his sensual lusts seemed to bring him success in life. This was not to dismiss his intelligence, which he considered more of an oarsman or perhaps a sail that aided the body in navigating the nebulous roads with their twists and turns and ups and downs, a bright mind that pushed him smoothly along as he encountered the beckoning feints and alluring falsehoods that were firmly planted in the enigmatic pupil of the world. He was young and handsome and healthy and had many friends and sufficient wealth and he felt happy and content, and consequently he reasoned that he had easily conquered all in life there was to conquer, and this gave him over to a slight disappointment that he had won so easily.

He had an easy smile and straight white teeth and towered over his brethren, and crystal-blue eyes that were his good fortune and pleasure seeds to anyone who gazed upon them;

and if one allowed these soul portals to penetrate one's natural barrier of distrust and settle inside one's fertile naivety, these azure sparklers would bloom the more he smiled and the more he talked in his smooth manner and flattering style, and thus he could seduce nearly anyone; and there was also the roundness of his head and face and the thickness of his blond hair, a symmetrical landscape, along with his naturally muscular body, which brought good vibrations of solace to onlookers who sought the company of physically and aesthetically superior life-forms.

So, this was his passageway to the inner and carefully guarded emotions of women everywhere, yet was also a lead into the secret society of men, who appreciated such a fine specimen either as friend or colleague, and who often felt somewhat superior in their own body as they stood in his inspiring shadow.

He had never labored very hard to be where he was because the physical laws of the world reward those bodies which possess an outer beauty that surpasses the natural order of genetic puzzle-making and are more in alignment with the masterfully woven tapestry that is Nature; it is true, he was more physically akin to a powerful oak tree or a shimmering galaxy or a majestic mountain, as his body seemed to have been carved over a long period of evolutionary time, above and beyond the puny, defective-looking bodies of his fellows; he was a walking, talking, breathing temple of Beauty to whom women happily sacrificed their bodies to experience, and whom men envied. It was in this way of leading with his physical prowess that he flourished and enjoyed all that the material world had to offer him—products and services he never, ever, not once, turned down.

He seemed to live in a world within a world, wrapped in a magical cloak that shielded him from life's incessant cuts and abrasions, even from the occasional catastrophe that befalls all residents of this planet; and yet, it must be stated that as he grew older and saw the monetary rewards of his neighbors, he began to lose some of his acquired happiness; and when he saw his colleagues gain promotions he thought he deserved, he began to acquire a small tide of bitterness; and although he had supreme health and a revolving harem of devastatingly gorgeous women, it all seemed wrong to him that others should prosper beyond his seemingly static wealth.

By the time he was thirty, he had married a woman of exceptional female beauty, and she had given him two beautiful children; yet he was becoming somewhat restless, which was very curious for someone who was born way ahead of the pack and given every opportunity to stay far, far ahead but who had always rested on the tenuous laurels of physical stature. He still had a good job but the money was merely mediocre to him, and he still had his health, but he wanted more now, more of what he was born with and more magnified now, and more of what he thought he deserved because people he knew and admired had more. You have it all, his wife sometimes said to him, holding up the baby, what else do you need? But he would merely shrug his burly shoulders and say that life was unfair because he wanted to experience all the luxuries that were afforded to men like him—men born of exceptional handsomeness and health and who had every good thing dropped at their feet and who had no natural barriers set before them because the world eagerly took them away.

In fact, he dreamed of having more of everything—more money, more women, a better job, a bigger house, influential friends, a finer cuisine, more of everything that stimulated his physical senses: all those things that his old mentor, his body, instructed him that he needed in order to fully survive and dominate in this mean ol' world. It was quite easy, he thought; if it makes you feel good, then it must be good for you. And so, he eventually received a promotion and ensnared a few mistresses and bought a bigger house and hired a maid and bought more of just about everything that he desired, and he looked around at the wide world and reasoned that he was as socially elevated as any man in his intimate circle. What more is there, he thought, when you have what you want in life?

But then one day a small visitor came to stay with him, an importunate rascal that took up residence deep within his still-handsome form. That certainly is odd, the man thought, upon awakening one morning, there is a dull ache in my back, I do not remember having done anything to strain it; but, oh well, it will go away, everything like that always does.

It was quite normal for him to think this way, for he had rarely been to the doctor, as his body always seemed to resist any illness that was traveling down the highly receptive human circuit; and so he continued on with his perfect life, feeling the silky, warm air kiss his bronze skin as he walked outside in the cool morning one day to his one-hundred-thousand-dollar cherry-red Porsche 911 Carrera GTS and then drove away toward work; and while driving he called his morning mistress and plied her with loves and kisses and promised her love and romance on the morrow; and later that night, on the drive home, he called his night mistress and plied her with loves and kisses and promised her love and romance on the weekend. His body was in a constant state of unbridled enthusiasm and rapture.

But this time, when he exited the car he felt the dull ache in his back flare up in a short burst of fiery pain, and he nearly

leapt off the ground, so unaccustomed was he to such discom-
fort; but as the pain did not follow him into the house, and
seemed, as the night progressed, to be an anomaly, he dismissed it, and by bedtime, he had completely forgotten that
it had ever existed.

Three months later, he was awoken by the same stabbing
pain in his lower back, and he rose up and jumped out of bed
and ran to the bathroom and lifted up his silk pajama and
peered at the troublesome spot but saw nothing and now felt
nothing; he went to the kitchen and poured some red wine
and drained it from the crystal glass and felt better and then
went back to bed and slept soundly that night. A week later,
the same pain announced its irksome presence while he was in
a meeting at work. This time he went to the doctor's office and
the doctor examined him and ordered tests but found nothing.
Probably just stress, the doctor with the quarter-million-dollar
smile said, and he said it smoothly because he, in fact, did not
have a piercing pain in his solid, one-hundred-percent-cov-
ered-by-insurance-forever back.

The pain continued to exert its presence in the man's back
more often and with more intensity. He visited the doctor
more often and the doctor ordered tests more often but the
tests always came back negative and the doctor always said
that perhaps the man just needed to rest or maybe take a holiday—more often.

So, the man and his family went on vacation to a faraway,
exclusive resort where ordinary-looking people with ordinary
means do not go, where the man fully expected the pain not
to follow him, just as if the pain was a perverted concept born
in the heat and smoke and suffering of the city and lay in the
minds and bodies of ordinary people but was a mistake in him
and not capable of asserting itself on a tranquil island with its

cerulean, pristine waters and people who were more like him in that they were born beautiful and who propagated their looks like purebred animals. The man was quite convinced that no bad thing could happen to him while he was amongst his own kind, these adorable, rich folk who lived a life of pleasure and ease and did not know what suffering was beyond looking for the dimpled white golf ball in the dense green thicket; but the pain did not have any such notions, nor cared about the company the man kept, and it seemed, once it struck him, to purposely come at times when he was communing with his own species, these gene-dominant, socially engineered, ultra-rich tycoons whom he idolized and worshipped just as if they were not fallible men and women but truly gods on earth.

The vacation was ruined and he was now in an ill humor because he could not have what he had always had, and that was complete and utter control of his body as it relates to harmony and solace; and if his body, the captain of him—the human ship—were in such a miserable and altered state, he could no longer interpret the proper signals it sent to steer him on the proper course. He was becoming perplexed.

It was fascinating how the invisible pain accelerated in its skillful voracity to assert itself as a dominant player in the life of the patient, his doctor mused as he consulted with his fellows; perhaps it is a parallel-psychological-pseudo-pain event, one that mirrors a common theme in the patient's life or is a plea for the patient to alter or preclude a particular activity, such as an affair the patient knows in his deepest psyche is wrong, or a crime, say, a blue-collar crime of embezzlement; our most sophisticated—and, let me add, expensive—examinations have failed to detect any organic origin for this phantom pain: no break in the tissue, no tumor, no disc degeneration, no muscle strain or pull—why, this patient is built like an immortal; every one of his vital signs are perfect and his body seems absolutely and perfectly...perfect. If all of our patients were this healthy, we might have to—ha!—start working for a living.

Thus, the man languished in this encroaching prison of pain without further assistance of the medical establishment; nor could he stabilize and subdue the filaments of pain as they invaded his thoughts and began to devour his equilibrium, for the structure of his mind was built on soft sand and incapable of spearing any malevolent advance toward it; thus, his brain allowed this marching army to invade its borders and seize the delicate hinges that kept it stable and sane and ignite the fiery torch to it and slowly melt them into an ashen heap; and as his emotional equilibrium crumbled, his mind directed this disintegration at those who meant the least to him; to wit, he cursed and denounced his mistresses and set them afloat to find another rich patron, and he cursed and denounced his colleagues and set them against him, and when he cursed and denounced his superiors, too, despite his long tenure at their company, they terminated him just as if his face had recently adorned the local post office bulletin boards.

So, his insular world was being peeled away from the thin outside coils to the thick, inner shield of layered gold, from the least important things and ideas and people to him and leading toward his crown jewel, his family, but his mind could not impede this malicious progress, for as the pain increased in magnitude and duration of attacks, he lost his endurance to resist punishing others for his failings. The pain was like a vicious worm unleashed inside his spirit and breaching his most private and heaviest protective psychological armor.

He felt like the man who is clinging to the side of a craggy cliff and loses his grip and falls a few feet but then manages to catch a jutting rock and holds on with bloody hands but feels his strength waning. The explosive spats with his wife over every little thing and interminable quarrels over every big thing formed the dagger that began to tear into her, and when he lost his job she cut ties with him and forced him out just like he had been a live-in gigolo-servant all their ten years together.

It seemed to him too remarkable that he had been born and then had lived until this point in his life without a stain upon his physical record, and even the relationship with his wife had been spectacular—even though he knew the account of the mistresses was certainly a misalignment, as he preached to himself the merits of his own self-aggrandizement, but hadn't he ripped out these bloodsuckers? And now because of the miserable pain, he was living in a humble apartment, thinking of what was and how it seemed it could never be the same again. Something was wrong, he knew, something was missing in his mental processes that would not allow him to design a line of analytical reasoning that would enlighten him as to the origin of the injury to his life. The doctors wanted to give him pain medication but he refused it because he knew that if the medicine burst into his outraged cells and soothed their fire, he would give up the quest to know what intellectual errors he had committed that had thrown him unceremoniously down to this unsteady and slippery societal rung.

It was a curious and yet courageous move for him to deny the acceptance of modern medicine to blunt his neurologically heightened sensory output, as it was his fleshly body that had been his champion and counselor and, indeed, benefactor, but as the fragile infrastructure of his mind was unraveling like a loose thread from a ball of yarn that was pulled by a playful kitten, it, this unadorned and practically naked mind, sought to know things it had been unrightfully deprived of;

and so, for the first time in its brief sojourn with the body of the man, it prevailed. Thus, the man was now a prisoner of his body and his mind, each of which were pulling mightily in opposite directions to free itself of this burden—like wild horses they were—and the man was squarely in the middle and being torn into mental chunks and pieces.

As the still-handsome and outwardly robust-looking man sat in the darkness of his sub-upper-class apartment and mused upon his fate, a small crack in the constant but invisible dam of knowledge that accompanies people began, and as it allowed a hiss and spurt of hot gas to erupt from its volatile waters, the man felt an undeniable break in the hardened calculus and scar tissue that had grown over his logical processes, to wit: he actually thought, just for the briefest time imaginable, that his wife had married him simply because she too was a disciple of the physical laws of the universe that proclaimed that those who were born in a rich broth of healthiness and covered in a rich paint of handsomeness are fated to mate with each other regardless of personality or intelligence, but he quickly dismissed this notion. Then, as his ailment prodded and poked him and smacked him up and down the crowded human boulevard of pain and suffering, he wondered why she had so readily accepted his wealth and actually encouraged him to work harder than ever and never seemed to mind when he was gone all day and night and was so eager to dismiss him from her life and take a bulk of his wealth. The more he deliberated upon this problem, the more curious he became, until he could take it no longer and did what many men do who have been ousted from the world of their spouse: he began to stalk her. It did not take long for him to find her with a man who, he soon found out, had been with her long before the dissolution of his own marriage. He lay in the hard shell of shock and awe for days, dead to the known sensory world except for his annoying resident and seemingly only companion now, pain.

Pain was his prime motivator now, pain that had settled in like a burrowing tic, pain that ripped and roared like a cracked whip against his feeble emotions, pain that eroded his will to engage in any activity not related to ameliorating this gruesome body snatcher.

He found, to his great consternation, that he no longer had friends, they having turned away from him once he was separated from his money and station in life. Could it be, the man thought, that they were mere acquaintances—conveniences, a contrivance—to further their own personal goals in life? He was astonished that he had such unkind thoughts, but as he examined the proof therein, he could find no other answer; and yet he was pleased that he had used his analytical processes to mine for such unfortunate conclusions. I am a lawyer, after all, he thought, massaging his sore back; there must be some good from my profession other than the taking of some poor fool's money.

The epicenter of pain remained the same but the spokes of the monster grew tendrils and they shot out far and wide and lightly flickered across his fleshly landscape; and once this mapping quest had been completed, tiny radials of tingling augured the coming of something more than wicked. But the man still refused medicine to quash the pain, for his mind, slowly unleashed from a cage built by ignorance, sought answers, and answers would not come, the man knew, if he was numb on mental anesthesia.

He could barely sleep at night, and so he would sometimes get up and go outside and walk about the city, and this brisk exercise seemed to alleviate his suffering. It was a community soaked in the finest riches, the benefits of this wealth apparent on every street with its exclusive shops and ornate homes, and draping every finely dressed citizen and adorning every finely crafted car. He wasn't certain what he was looking for, but he instinctively knew that traversing this diamond-encrusted, ruby-layered playground of penthouses and palaces would not provide any answers he sought; so, one night, he boldly walked past the borders of his shining kingdom and penetrated the parallel world of reality.

People stared at him. He took out his vanity mirror and checked his face and then examined his clothes and everything seemed in order; but the staring continued, and so dismayed was he that he soon found a street sweeper and confronted the man about the staring habits of the citizens herein, whereupon the man sort of frowned and smiled and then said: hey, buddy, you're wearing clothes that would take these folks a year to buy, at which point the sweet sweeper in his steel monolith carried on his morning duties.

The man looked about himself and raised up his two-thousand-dollar, handmade Berluti brown leather shoes, and screwed up his eyes, and then grabbed hold of his one-thousand-five-hundred-dollar Brunello Cucinelli snowflake cashmere sweater that had been handmade in Italy, and he looked around at the people in their humble attire. Well, thought the man, they need to work harder for what they want in life; it is not my fault they live like they do. The man then hurried home, as his journey into the land of the commoners had unsettled him. There are no answers there, he thought to himself as he stared at his still-handsome self in the bathroom mirror; that town is a town that is made for people who need to be there, just as this town is made for people who need to be here. He shrugged his shoulders, and thought, it is the way it is; people come to be where they are through their own actions, and is not for me to consider.

Despite the scraping away of his sanity by the pain, he still needed to work, and so he joined a prestigious law firm in town, but they soon let him go because his physical limitations would not allow him to dedicate his days and nights to cases; and after being terminated by four more such firms, he eventually found work in a small firm that specialized in helping the poor. The pay was meager and the work was undemanding but his superiors and colleagues seemed to appreciate his legal expertise. His first case involved a woman who had been injured while on the job, and he visited her at her house on a Saturday morning.

Her home was small but clean, and it smelled of the freshly made bonds of family and the aroma of love, and as the man conversed with the badly broken woman in her wheelchair, he observed that she was always smiling and hugging her children and extolling the virtues of her life; and she spoke of how she had nothing to complain about, that she was happy and content no matter how the trial turned out, and she said it did not matter because she had her husband and her children and her beautiful house and many friends and relatives who loved her and that was all she needed. It made no sense to him that she could utter such ideas while bound and braced to physical imperfection.

But wouldn't life be better if the accident had never happened at all, he asked her, to which she replied, why, yes, of course, but having my body in pain could never take away the real joys in her life, because if that were so, then the joys of the world would rest on physical purity, and that, she said, would be an unpleasant place to be.

As he drove home in his Porsche, he mused upon the words of the woman but he did not understand them at all. How can one be happy, he wondered, if the body is in agony, for agony brings a dissolution of mind and spirit, and then it is better to die.

He was to see many more such clients and most of them were in the general state of happiness as the woman, and this perplexed the man, and as his pain grew and his mind shattered, the idea of happiness in a wrecked body made him vexed. Health is one of the greatest achievements in life, he said one day in his apartment, but then he pondered this statement, as he had never uttered such a thought before. What could it all mean? he wondered.

His mind was fracturing as surely as a small boat in a storm that is crashed against the jagged rocks and splinters to pieces. He quit his job. He lost his apartment. He sold his car. He moved to another town and found a small pad and therein he dwelled like a monk in a temple, listening to the music of his pain fill his senses and blow out his mind with its bellowing and boastful trumpeting. He knew salvation was nigh, salvation in the blessed form of medicine to quell the horrible pain, but the images of the injured people and their inner tranquility, and the idea of health now being so important, grabbed hold of him and shook him and implored him to listen, to hear its lyrical song, a composition the man knew he would never hear with the illusory gifts the happy endorphins from drugs would bring.

He did not know why but he began to visit hospitals and simply walk onto wards where the patients with the worst illnesses resided; and therein he would listen to the conversations they had with their kin, and he was amazed, for he heard no bitterness, no envy, no strife, no complaining of lost privileges, no desires to go back and begin again, no memories of just the good times—no, the conversations he heard spoke of joy and love and the strength of the family and relatives and friends and how they would bring succor to one another, and many times the patients were offering comfort to those not crippled, not diseased, not dying, and he was amazed; yet, the only time he was not amazed was when he saw people alone and covered in their silent misery, and therein he recognized himself and felt great sorrow for them, and for many of them, he even visited and attempted to placate their suffering.

He knew now that health was very important, but knew that ill health must not preclude one from enjoying life; he still did not fully understand it but he acknowledged its conceptual existence, and began to wonder if people actually loved one another despite poverty and physical ugliness and conflicts. Can it be so, he wondered, that such people exist in life, and that I have not seen this? He felt as if his mind was now being tuned to a different beat.

When he chanced to look into the mirror six months hence, he was aghast because the image that was relayed back to him was frightening; his thick blond hair had become thin and his muscles had begun to atrophy and his rugged face had lost its comely profile. I look like I belong in another place, he murmured, but then wondered what other place he meant, for he was already living in a town he considered a very different place.

On a caprice he bought a ticket and boarded a place and soon found himself at the resort he had visited with his family; and for every moment he was there, someone was staring at him, and not with stares of stealth and politeness that are craftily veiled, but brutal stares, bold stares, the what-in-the-name-of-all-that-is-decent kind of stares that one gets when one is far afield of one's established status in life. Were these not his own kind, he wondered, as the people there frowned and groped him with their haughty looks; was our connection only money and looks? Are these people no more than empty vessels who fill themselves with mammon and cover their massaged and oiled bodies with hot mud and scented blossoms to pretty their flesh and thus separate themselves from the real world? Perhaps, he wondered, they are not real, but mere fabrications that should not be considered at all. Is it possible, he mused, on the flight back home, that he was—had been—one of them?

When he arrived home, he burst into his apartment and found himself joyous to be there and not in the clutches of those supercilious aristocrats, and he laughed at this despite his pain, and when he felt his pain he actually laughed at it, and for a brief moment, it failed to usurp his emotions. He smiled, the first smile he had had in months. A victory once, he whispered, is a victory that can be had again, if you know what you are fighting for.

As he lay in bed that night, he felt as if he were becoming someone else, as if his soul was awakening and commencing to brush clean the layers of debris that had encrusted over it. Is it yet possible, he thought, lying there in the sweltering heat he did not mind, and on a small, soft bed he did not mind, that I have never been truly happy, and that what I believed was happiness was really an absence of suffering? So, are the only happy people the ones not in pain? And what of those people I have met, what of them and their sufferings? Where have I been, he whispered, beginning to weep, and who was I, and will I become the man I need to be in order to understand the world and experience real joy?

He felt an anxious want to deliver himself from what he had been but he realized it could not be accomplished unless he visited his old life. So, presently, there he was, standing in the soft shadows of the perfectly manicured trees and bushes as he watched his beautiful wife and her beautiful fiancé stroll down the driveway of the home he had designed in his own exquisite image; they certainly are exceptional, he thought, and imagined himself there amongst them and be shook his head and realized that he would have to be the washed pig that goes back to wallow in the mud; what he did next he could not presently explain, but he slowly stepped from the safe darkness and walked toward the couple and revealed himself in plain sight; the face of the woman blanched horror and the face of the fiancé gnawed on shock, and then the face of the woman frowned and bled sympathy, while the face of the man sneered and evinced amusement and pity. The man just stood there and stared at them, and asked about his daughters and asked when he could see them, to which the woman, still flustered and embarrassed and, more importantly, ashamed she had ever been conjoined with this man, responded that they were fine, and yes, he could see them soon.

Now, the man knew why he done this terribly brave thing, he had wanted to see his children, his own flesh and blood he had never considered these past months and now knew that he loved more than his own misbegotten life. Am I yet to be a man, he wondered, walking away from the still unsettled couple; am I yet to be a real person, truly real? Is it too late? Might a man redeem himself from the gutter or is a man lost forever once he corrupts his own soul? He wept all the way home and he did not care who saw him.

The pain was boring into his skull now like a steel spike that is lined with dynamite and is blown up every second and sends incendiary fragments of misery that cuts a corrugated path along his nerve fibers; it clenched its steel teeth and chewed on his waning fortitude and he was indeed bowing to it. His whole body stung and ached and throbbed and begged for rest from persecution, but he would have none of it. I must go deeper still, he knew, so I might die a man and not a decoration, an unconscious creature conceived in bigotry and arrogance, a blight, a sore on society—I must die a man or I was never born at all. And it was in this way that he welcomed the pain and negotiated with it to leave him alone so it might allow him to pursue what was important to him before he died.

When he visited his children and held them next to his anguished and emaciated body, they did not seem to mind; when he hugged them and kissed them and told them how much he loved them, they did not seem to care what he looked like, for he was their father, and they could feel his genuine love and they could freely give their innocent love to him. So, while he was away from them he could think only of the time when he would be with them again, and when he thought of them, his pain subsided. It is apparent, the man thought, that sometimes one does not have to negotiate or scrape before pain in order to subdue it, one has only to live, but to live properly in the world and not apart from it; yes, the man whispered as he stared into the mirror of reality—not knowing that the worldly scales that had covered his eyes for so long were slowly falling away from him with every passing day—before, I was dead, and now I am alive, and the pain will soon learn who is the master and who is the slave of this body.

He went back to work and volunteered for the most difficult cases involving the clients with the worst physical hardships. He was able to control the pain at times with his mind and other times the pain would simply recede as he talked in earnest with these people whose lives should have been slain by pain but who somehow had rerouted their river of suffering until it was submissive to them and set upon trampling it asunder

every time they cared for someone and every time they per-
formed a good deed. It was in this way that the man learned
about self-sacrifice and humility, and when he set about to do
such acts, he felt a tingling of gladness in his heart, for doing
such things that had nothing to do with mammon or physical pleasure or personal gain was a new sensation for him. So,
he thought, after observing a man who was blind in one eye
and nearly blind in the other spend his entire day coordinat-
ing efforts to help a friend in need, this is life, this is living;
I was dead, and I did not know it; and now I am alive, and
how much more have I to learn? For I am as a baby, taking
my first steps, and learning the mysterious ways of the world.

He would spend as much time as he could now with his
children and was always sure to be there for them any time
they needed him and be where they needed him to be; he now
knew that nothing must sever this sacred tie to his precious
daughters, for to lose them now would mean to lose all that
he had gained, which was life itself. Joy was a seed that grew
in him and blossomed and spread warmth over his rejuve-
nating heart.

He was driving home one day from work and he noticed
a slender woman having great difficulty getting out of her car
in a parking lot. He drove up to her and offered his services
and soon helped her into her wheelchair and then escorted
her into the grocery store. He learned that she had been in a
car accident and that she was in physical therapy. He took her
back to her car and after putting her groceries on the backseat,
he helped her inside and bid her farewell. The next day at the
same time he saw her struggling once again to safely exit her
small blue sedan and once again he came to her aid, and this
time, after helping her shop and bringing her back to her car,
he asked to see her again, to which she hesitated and replied

that she would think about such an important proposition. He watched her drive away and realized that he knew practically nothing about her. A week later he saw her again and she accepted his kind offer of dinner.

She was a widow and a mother of three children, she said, and related to him how she had worked her entire life, how the accident had occurred, and how she wondered why he was still in his seat after she had told him this. He smiled at the woman with the naturally long brown hair and soft brown eyes and told her about his life and then said that he was the lucky one here and wondered why she did not leave, to which she smiled and said that he was the most handsome man she had ever seen. He blushed, something he had never done, ever; he did not understand this, he said to her, how he could appear handsome to her, and then she reached out and placed her small hand underneath his jutting chin and gazed deeply into his still-lustrous blue eyes and said that she could indeed see into his noble soul. No one had ever called him good, ever. I do not understand why we are talking thus, he said to her, we barely know each other; to which she replied, but our souls recognized each other instantly, and it is for this reason that we can communicate so easily, as we are the same person, though from different places and long ago wearing different guises but now united in one spirit. He did not believe it because it frightened him.

A month hence and he realized he was truly in love with her, and now he was frightened more than ever because he felt inferior to her, this woman who never complained about her fate, this mother who selflessly raised three children, this woman who kept a loving and clean home. One day he was at that immaculate home and he was talking to the eldest daughter, and she asked him if he knew about the operation, to which he replied that he did not. Well, the teenager began, the operation might help heal her mother, but the cost was too much and her family had no insurance.

The man was shocked that the woman had never mentioned the operation to him, and he cogitated upon this omission for days, and finally decided that this woman was a real woman, unlike all of the women he had ever known who always had a hand out for themselves but never had a hand in to help anyone else. He understood now that she would not ask him because she did not want him to think that she was using his relationship for money, as people often do. At times like this, the pain was not even felt in him, as if it were a distant memory of something long ago and experienced by another person but now conquered and cut in twain and buried.

Six months later and he was at the home of the woman and he was the guest of honor at the dinner table and telling amusing stories to the three girls who now loved him like he was their own father; and then he told a story about a great woman who had worked honestly her entire life and who dealt honestly with people and never asked for anything in return because she thought it was best for her and best for the world if the world was to be a better place. And then the man threw down a manila envelope and asked the woman to look inside of it, to which she readily assented, and when she read the paper therein, her face grew handsome and her heart radiated so much love that the people felt it, therein. But what does this mean, she asked, clutching her bosom, an operation, this cannot be, I have no money for this.

He smiled and held her hand and winked at the children who knew what was to come because they had helped him plan the whole thing. The operation will happen when you want it because of who you are, because that is the way the world works, he said, you have taught me that much; those in need who help others in need will have their needs taken care of; and darling, O darling, you have met my needs and the needs of your wonderful daughters and those you help at the homeless shelter and everyone else who loves you and wants this for you; so, my beautiful angel, you will now have that operation because there is a great deal of money in the world that is so often stored in too large a sum in too few hands, and sometimes it is necessary and even fitting and proper to redistribute some of that money into the hands of those who need it more than those who do not even know how much they hoard. He smiled, then, knowing that she loved him and that he loved her, and that her children loved them both; and he knew he was twice blessed because he had his own children whom he loved and who loved him. He was sitting in the temple of love now and he could think of nothing but helping this selfless woman before him.

And after he married her and began a life with the three daughters and his own two daughters, he never again thought about the pain that begged for attention and squealed for embrace and could not exist without the explicit request and collusion of the host body, this pain that existed in the minds and hearts of people who cannot see anything other than or beyond their own flesh; and for those who make their flesh a holy shrine, any imperfect sensation is heightened and hoisted up into the greatest importance until it takes over the mind as well as the heart and remains there until the human being therein learns what is more important in life than the adoration of the body.

-Finis-

The Vanishing Point

Vindictive accusations crawled out of his screaming mouth and consumed her timid body like a boiling, rising tide; bitter imprecations flew out of his distraught brain with the precision of champion archers and pierced her wounded psyche so often that there were no fresh places left to strike her; insidious maledictions launched from his cunning spirit to cast a steel net over her shrinking form. It must be understood that she did not suffer this harsh criticism because of a great error she had made or anything she had done against him—no, it was something he had done himself, but he needed to pin her against the wall with the hot wind coming out of his yawning red mouth and blast her small frame into submission to atone for his own sins. He had to know his verbal cannon hit its target or his wrath would increase, and she had to be the one to accept this inglorious assemblage of mean and nasty words because she was his wife.

Transliteration of his linguistic style is necessary now, for even the most ardent practitioner of foul language would blush and turn aside upon hearing how often and for what little purpose and for how long he uttered such gross profanities; and he even used normal words like a sharp scalpel to chop and slice and dig emotional wounds and cuts and abrasions into his audience. Now, it must be stated at the onset that even though the wife was the main recipient of this oral carnage, he did attempt to hold these word daggers over a hot flame and then fling them against strangers or acquaintances, but most often, the people merely blew him off just as if he were a teeny-tiny bug who was making faces at them from atop a teeny-tiny red brick wall; however, there were some people who were forced to put up with his ill humor, and this was because he was an artist of considerable renown.

Before an honest transliteration begins, however, a brief presentation shall first be given so the reader might appreciate just how often the man used these corrosive words—hard, hurtful words that are not necessary to convey meaning or exist for any good thing, but instead should be buried deep, deep in the back of a spooky, foggy swamp—such words that will now be exchanged with that most innocuous of adjectives, "silly."

In addressing his wife one morning, the following tirade fairly exploded out of his gaping mouth: "You silly silly stupid son-of-a-silly stupid silly, didn't I tell you to get the silly paint from the silly cabinet and mix the silly colors the silly way I told you, you silly, silly, silly, silly idiot! You silly idiot, do I have to do every silly thing around this silly place!" There was a small pause here so he might catch his panting breath, the same way a boxer might after a flurry of punches against a strong rival. "You silly son-of-a-silly silly woman, why, why did I marry you, you silly silly silly no-good-for-nothing silly silly…" As it is plain to see that he treated these unclean words as if they were as common as dirt, it is now appropriate here to interject the Latin phrase "ad infinitum."

So, with that out of the way, let the compete transliteration begin!

No one slept if he was up, and no one was up while he slept; this decree described the philosophy of the man when it came to dealings with his wife, to wit: whatever he was doing, she too must be doing, or there would be great wrath for her to incur; however, even if she attempted, with the utmost sincerity and humility, exactly what he wanted her to do, she incurred his great wrath, anyway.

"Get in here, you idiot!" he cried to her one very early morning, a cold morning where even the sleepy stars were rudely awakened by his ridiculous tantrums, "and bring the palette right now!"

She was a small woman with fine, long brown hair and a kind face and small brown eyes and a normally slow walk that accelerated whenever he polluted the air with his oily commands. "Yes, Norman," she said, walking into the studio room with the wooden palette and then setting it down on his steel, gray desk.

He looked over at her and his face grew furious and his tone grew exasperated, just as if he had been instructing someone else—like a ten-year-old child or an indentured slave—for months on how to set up his studio. "Put the palette," he shouted, as if he were talking to a person who for the first time had just acquired the miracle of hearing and who was also learning English, "on the easel!"

"Yes, Norman," she said, respectfully, not daring to say that he had wanted the palette on the steel desk the last two days and the palette on the easel the two days before that.

He ran his short, slender fingers through his brown, curly hair and walked over toward her, his gait graceful, his arms swinging carefully at his sides—as he considered himself an artist even when he walked and when he held his hands while gesturing and even when he held his head when speaking. "Now, get the pastels," he said, somewhat appeased now, and brushed against her for no reason other than to remind her of his looming physical presence. She carefully removed the pastels from the cabinet and the brushes and charcoal from the drawers and laid them out all very nicely on the steel desk and then stood quietly awaiting instructions; however, when he saw this unfortunate transgression—where she thought for herself and anticipated his next action—he went, plainly, berserk. "Did I ask you to get out the brushes, did I? Did I tell you to get the charcoal and place it right here?" he violently screamed, so hard that the palette on the easel vibrated. "Did I, you worthless piece of human real estate!" He glanced in the mirror to see if his head was in the proper "attack position" and if his hands were circulating in an artistic fashion, and then he continued his verbal barrage, akin to a field gunner—his mind being the gunner that loaded the hot-boiling bullets and his mouth being the steel cylinder that spat out the fiery projectiles. "Now, put it all back right now!" Yet, she might have been surprised had she just then heard his most intimate thoughts, for he was going to tell her to lay out precisely the same tools she had laid out, but he was angry because she had done it without his explicit command and that she had done it correctly; it was his belief that she could do nothing right unless he directed her to do it, and if she did something right without his consent, it was certainly due to happenstance and not some sort of intelligence, as he considered her gender to possess the lowest form of intelligence on the planet—actually, his planet, where every man was above every woman in every category of life.

When this small episode was over, she merely stood there awaiting his next command; if she chose to sit, he ordered her to stand; if she stood, he ordered her to sit; if she asked if he were hungry, he shouted that he would tell her if he was; if she did not ask him, he berated her for not doing so. He would work all day in the studio and expect her to be there all day with him, and if she asked to do something for herself, he would hem and haw and throw a fit, even if the act she was requesting benefitted both of them.

"Norman, may I go shopping now? We are all out of food," she politely asked about noontime.

He dramatically dropped his brushes and noticed in the mirror how his posture was, and he decided he liked how his body was juxtaposed with the diffused light coming through the high window, and made a mental note of the effect; nevertheless, he turned toward her, exasperated, and said, "Do I have to tell you to go shopping when we have no food?" and he pointed to his head, and in doing so, splashed some paint on his hair, which burst another ever-present, wrath-filled balloon above him. "See what you made me do, you imbecile!" And when she attempted to clean up this paint on him, he pushed her away. "Go away, go ruin someone else's life for a change, I need a break from you."

When she was in the car, she noted the mileage and wrote it down in her little black book, and wrote down the time, too, and then sped off down the road helter-skelter.

The first call on the cell phone came at twelve-thirty in the p.m., and he demanded that she describe the scenery she was driving past, which she accurately did, at which point he hung up on her; at twelve-fifty in the p.m., her cellphone rang and he demanded that she describe the foodstuff in the aisle that contained the canned soups and meats, and after he compared the items she accurately described to the video he had recently made of that same aisle, he abruptly hung up on her.

When she returned home, he stormed out of the studio room, still wearing his beige cotton painter's coat, and first came to the car and looked at the mileage and the time on his watch and then compared it to his little black book of statistics; and once inside the house grabbed the grocery receipt out of her hand and then one by one took out each item in the brown paper bags and compared them to the dollar and cents amount on the receipt. He let out a loud "hrumph" when he realized that all of the figures matched. "Fix me lunch!" he growled and then went back to his precious work.

The meal she prepared for him was delectable beyond words, yet no good thing came out of his mouth about it; he would not condemn the fine cuisine she had so expertly delivered to him, for she was as great an artist in the kitchen as he was an artist in the studio; but he would never praise it, either, for he thought she needed no commendations for something she had been commissioned by Nature to perform, and certainly did not want her to think he needed or appreciated her in any way; but more importantly, he reasoned that every time he praised her for something good she did, it would diminish every great thing he accomplished.

At three o'clock in the p.m., he was unhappy with the way his charcoal painting was coming, so he heaved the easel through the window; this is what he did, unlike the average frustrated citizen who does not outrun that great pauser, reason, he outran it every time; and every time he felt like picking up a particular weighty object and hurling it at something or someone, he did it, because, he reasoned, he was who he was and he had certain privileges commoners would never have or deserved to have. He was, as has been stated, an artist of great renown, and had decided he was not subject to the same laws, either manmade or natural, as the rest of humanity—he may be one of them in physical body, he often thought, but his mind was not their mind, not like their reptilian-mammalian brain that was just a peasant's brain dressed in modern clothing.

As it was, she called the glass man to come and clean up the mess, and then she fixed her husband another sumptuous meal and watched as he slowly raised his alcohol level with white wine and then witnessed his personality soften like an old, leather rag that is massaged with a rich, unrefined olive oil; it was then that he might hug her and hold her for a few seconds, it was then that he might not scream and shout at her, it was then that he forgot about her as he lay in his dense fog on the sofa while watching the mindless images on the television screen; and it was then that she lived, the only way she could—by reading and calling her friends and relatives and reassuring them that everything was all right.

This was how it was, this was how she survived, this was one of the secrets to her success with the man that popular and scholarly magazines called the most irascible, tyrannical and most important artist of his generation.

And then one day he quit drinking.

She never knew why it came or how it came about, but one day he just did not pour himself that bubbly white wine and instead took to the studio again and barked for her presence; and just like that, she lost her emotional equanimity. Her friends, when she secretly met with them after this, and her relatives, when she secretly called them after this, admonished her of the consequences of staying with him, but she always reassured them that everything would be all right. "I will do the right thing and honor my wedding vows and do my wifely duties and be the good suffering servant and win him over," she would tell them, and despite their most fervent protestations, she did not yield nor bend nor break her vow.

He had invaded her head and invaded her body but she had always found paradise at night, but now that it was sealed off from her, she was slowly slipping toward a mental oblivion, for there was no rest from his omnipresent personality, which followed her even to the bathroom, where she had to shout her name every one minute, as he feared she might be heading out the window therein; and there was no fleeing his long reach by his denial for her to attend the funerals of friends and the funerals of relatives and the marriages of friends and the marriages of relatives and the births of babies of friends and relatives; she did nothing unless it benefitted him, and she knew it and she knew she would never walk out of that door because she still believed in the sanctity of marriage and had promised to stay with him forever. She was condemned and she had condemned herself; so, she could talk to no one about it because it was by her own free will that she stayed. The noose had tightened tighter, and she was suffocating slowly and knew where the precious oxygen was but would not inhale it.

This went on for ten more years.

His fame increased beyond the expectations of any art critic, and his paintings became the highest-priced works of art in the world. He could do whatever he wanted and be with whomever he pleased, but he only wanted to stay in his home and keep his wife-servant-concubine; he did not care about the money or the fame, and in this way, he truly was an artist. There was a little gray in his goatee now but he was still young, and even though he was as tightly wound as a stretched rubber band all the day and night, his health was supreme; and even though she was still young, her health was failing, and she often had fevers and falls, and terrible colds and hacking coughs that he often berated her for. She caught every virus in its virulent cycle and every cold that was available; her immune system was like a cracked windshield that is covered by bugs and filth and that lets in every kind of pollution and ill wind.

He was slowly encroaching on her private sanctuaries. He was intrusive now in the kitchen, where he criticized her cooking and how she cleaned the dishes and how she arranged the pots and pans; he had her landline phone calls monitored and he had a tracking device placed inside her cell phone; and now, despite his immense fame and accompanying fortune, he was still scrutinizing her shopping habits and examining the bills she brought home. He spent many long nights interrogating her on her particular purchases and belittling her for her poor choices; consequently, he decided to accompany her on her journeys to the local stores.

Upon hearing the news of his newest decree, she lay like one dead for a week. "He cannot do this," she mused, unable to lift her hands to massage her throbbing head, "he cannot invade the only place left where I find solace; he cannot do such a thing, I must tell him that I need to have at least this time to myself, he must listen…"

She timidly walked up to him the morning of his avowed threat to accompany her to the grocery store. "Norman," she began, hesitantly, "I want to talk to you…"

He turned round from reading the morning newspaper and scowled at her. "What have I told you about starting off with a sentence 'I want, I want,'" and he made childish faces to accentuate his position; "just get to the point, you don't need a preface every time you open your stupid mouth, I don't have the time for it," and when she didn't speak, he threw down the newspaper in exasperation. "What is it, what, what?"

"Norman, I do not think you need to go with me to buy groceries."

"Well," he said, nearly smiling, "that wasn't hard to do, now was it?" and he placed his hairy arm around her small shoulders. She felt hopeful. His voice was calm and reassuring. "In the future, speak like that—direct and to the point—and oh, by the way, I couldn't care less what you think, so gather your irritating female crap and get in the car and have the engine going by the time I get out there." He kissed her and walked away, whistling.

He criticized everything she did as she drove, yelling at her to step on the brakes or quit riding the brakes or speed up or slow down or turn here or turn there, but finally they pulled into the local shopping parking lot and were soon in the grocery store. Every aisle they went down, he had a lecture ready for her on how to save money; and for every item he picked up and held before her, he expected her to write down notes on how to select the item in the future.

"See this here," he said, his voice too loud for his close proximity to her, "this brand of toilet paper is not a good buy." She was blushing as she looked around at the staring customers. "Hey," he shouted, grabbing hold of her head and steering it toward the items in question, "concentrate on the task at hand," and he shook his head with a stern look upon his countenance; "don't you worry about what other people think about you," and he pointed to his barrel chest, "you need to worry about me." He was glaring right into her eyes, just as if he wished his stare could pierce into her brain and restructure it completely. "This brand," he said, slowly, and held up the offending toilet paper roll, "is the crap you always get—no more," he shouted, and he thrust his hand over her head, "get it!" She attempted to speak but he shut her mouth with a shout, and then said, "Look at the amount of sheets per roll on this one!" He pushed her round head forward until her face was nearly squished into the plastic package. "Can you read? It says that there are only two hundred and fifty sheets per roll; now, look at the price per quantity here," and he pushed her head toward the hard plastic sticker under the products, "you are paying way too much; now," and her raised her head toward another brand, "see this one, you idiot, it has three hundred and fifty sheets per roll," and then he pushed her head down again, "and the price per quantity is cheaper." She attempted to speak but he demanded her silence, promising much emotional torment if she dared to speak again.

"Sir," a strong voice declared, spearing the interaction of the man and woman, "you need to leave."

Norman looked up and beheld an ordinary-looking woman in an ordinary-looking store uniform, and when he realized she had very little authority, he sneered at her and said, "You need to leave," and then waved his hand toward her. "Shoo, shoo, go clean up a spill or something—or maybe, go eat a donut and be happy."

But she did not possess an ordinary mind, and easily repulsed his demeaning attacks. "I have already called for security to come and escort your rude manners out of here." She said it without any emotional tumult or apprehension.

"Do you know who I am, you stupid peon?"

"No, don't you?"

"I am Norman Rotweiller," he fairly screamed, holding up his hand as if in a pose, "the greatest artist in the world!"

"That's nice," she returned, just as if he had announced that he was the first Martian to visit Earth, "because in here, you're just another house-husband-shopper, and you obey our rules," and then she turned and smiled as she saw the two burly security men coming toward her, and she presently instructed them to take only the man away, despite his vehement orders to take his wife, too; and when he was gone, the woman turned to Jean, for that was her name, and said, with great compassion, "Do you ever wonder what they dream about in the greatest dream that is Heaven?" And her simple smile enlarged as she watched the gentle face of Jean light up and evince gratitude, and then Jean, weeping, embraced the woman, and then hurried out toward the car, knowing full well that she would experience much sorrow and grief for this incident.

That night, Norman, the invincible—as if truly he were built of a finer stuff than the mere stuff of his fellows, the man who never was sick but, according to all of the dictates of modern science, should have exploded long ago and left his flesh and bone fragments scattered all over the house—became feverish; and his wife attended to him like a good wife, sitting next to him all night long and holding his hand and wiping his sweaty forehead. Five days later, the fever broke.

She was in the kitchen fixing a good breakfast when she first heard his cry, and she came running into his room to see his face shedding waves of terror. "What has happened, what has happened? Call a doctor, call one now, for I cannot see!"

She could not suppress her thrilled feelings of hope, and she tried to feel ashamed, but it did not come. "You cannot see?" she asked, not able to hide her desire for his positive response, and when he called her an imbecile for her question, she did not feel badly at all, but then he did say something even more curious.

"I cannot see color! I am ruined! I see the world as mere mortals must see it!"

She was somewhat depressed but still she felt elated and curiously powerful. "I will call the doctor." She walked away, not even hearing his ranting and raving.

After extensive testing of Norman's eyes by the doctor of internal medicine and the eye specialist, it was determined that the fever had brought on a specific condition called cerebral achromatopsia, or more commonly called color blindness, even though they could find nothing organically wrong with the cones of his eyes. Norman refused to listen to this verdict and argued with both doctors but found he could not dissuade them from their diagnosis; and after six more months of expensive testing, he capitulated and accepted his fate.

He sulked around the house, murmuring to himself and shouting outrage against the unseen fates. "What is a color!" he shouted at his wife every day. "What is color, for I cannot see it, I cannot feel it, I cannot remember it—I cannot even see it in my head! The whole world is an abysmal gray and a rotting black and a dirty white—you must be my color eyes!" She felt honored to help him.

His paintings had been known for their vibrant colors and contrasting hues and specific color placement, and now, when he painted—when he dared use the color schemes—the colors were a nebulous mush, a child's rendering of choice, a blur of color that smothered the painting, but of course, he did not know this; and when he attempted to sell these paintings, no one wanted them, and he cursed his wife and so directed her to fill in the palette with only those colors he could see, and he painted the world as he saw it—dreary, filthy, faded—and these paintings were not sold and his reputation was impugned even further. "But I am the king!" he would shout upon hearing of the failure to sell his work. "Tell me what the critics are saying," he demanded of her one day, and ordered her to read an article he had specifically picked out.

She began to read the essay with an imperceptible glimmer of glee. "'It appears that those people who decide what is art and what is not, what is good and what is bad, who is a great artist and who is not—the art galleries and the art critics and the rich patrons—have now decided that Norman Rotweiller is no longer one of the gods whose hands have been dipped in the magical pool of talent—a fate befitting a man who was allowed to subject patrons and gallery owners and critics with the greatest disdain, a man who…'"

Norman tore the newspaper from her hands and ripped it apart and threw it back at her. "Why would you read that one, you little fool!"

She wasn't sure why but she found herself silent when he was driving her to the grocery store the next day and about to run a red light—red was black as coal now to his eye palette and so was green, and yellow was no better than a light gray—and since he was like most people who never bothered to worry about the color order of the light signals, he just wasn't thinking about any of it; but then she would say at the last second that the light was red and he would reluctantly slam on the brakes and then berate her.

One day, after such an episode, she blurted out, without meditating upon the consequences of the overt semantics of the statement, "Why don't you just memorize the order of light signals; other color blind people do." She gasped when she realized her error, but she had felt this intense urgency inside her to speak, and felt that she could not repress it.

He screamed at her just as if she had described his mother as a downtown, lascivious streetwalker-prostitute-gun runner—the same biography he did often sketch about his mother. "How dare you tell me that, after all the things I have done for you—you can't do one little thing for me, like tell me when to stop and when to go?"

She was silent and looking straight ahead and wondering why she was still in the car with him. She brushed back her long brown hair and looked at the man in the car next to them and smiled at him and he smiled back. "I am still young," she said aloud, and flinched when she realized she had once more loosed words through her tight lips.

"What does that mean, you little trollop?" He had witnessed the interaction between her and the man. "Are you saying you are going to leave me now that I am an invalid?"

"No," she returned, shocking herself again, as she never responded more than once or twice in a row to his commands and queries, "but I am your wife and I do want your respect, especially now that you need me more than ever." She quickly clasped her hands to her mouth as her eyes opened wide in astonishment.

He smashed the car to the curb and slammed open his door and ran to her side and yanked open her door and physically pulled her out of the car and then banged the door shut and quickly walked back to his side and got in the car and drove away at a high speed.

She was watching him with wonder as he drove away, and she was thinking that if there was any justice in the world, then he would crash the car right now, right in front of her, not a year from now, not ten years from now—nor must he be like the infuriating drunk who drives the windy and icy roads and every other kind of road for fifty years and never receives a ticket and never crashes; no, he must crash now, she thought, as she watched him speed through the first yellow light and then speed on to the next intersection; and when the blue sedan was nearly out of view, she saw it, yes, she plainly saw it smash into another car and she heard a second later the thud and thunder of the two cars waltzing down the sparking pavement. She started walking toward the incident, feeling as if this was the time of her, as if her life was about to begin anew, as if she had done the right thing but now that was over and she would be free to live again, and that she deserved it, too. She came upon the crash and told the police officer who she was, and as she got into the ambulance with Norman, she whispered to him his as she watched his shaking, sweaty body, "I will ride with you as I should, as a dutiful wife should; but I will tell you now that you must presently love me, or you will be alone with your crimes." She no longer cared why she was allowing her innermost thoughts to translate to spoken words. He made no reply.

The doctor said that Norman had sustained only a concussion. When Norman awoke in the hospital bed, the first thing he did was pull his hand away from hers, and after clearing his head and eating a full meal, he unleashed his arsenal of malice with both barrels. "It's all your fault, you should have been in the car with me—why couldn't any of this have happened to you—why, why me, who has never hurt anybody, who has a unique gift to share with the world?"

Instead of her simply listening and playing the mute fool, she interjected, throwing his babbling brain off balance and knocking him off a rhythm he had mastered over the decades.

"You are merely a man, like every other man; you are no more important than any other man or any other person because of your monetary success and fame in the world of art; and you are certainly a mean man, as it is expressed by the way you treat others—but here I do not include myself because I have stayed with you out of a sense of duty and honor—I am your wife, and so I cannot regard myself as someone you disdain." He was so aghast that his spongy red tongue was riveted to his closed, dry mouth. "I have loved you despite your cruelty to me, and am willing to stay with you if you are willing to be as you once were, when we met so long ago, when you did not so despise the world."

He screamed and reached for her arms and pulled her toward him. "My vision is going, I cannot see everything around me—the outer edges of the room are disappearing—help me, you must help me!"

"I will help you, I will, for I am your wife, and dedicated to you, but you first must say, with all of your heart and mind and spirit, that you will treat me with the respect accorded to a wife."

"Help me, help me," he shouted, his eyes darting everywhere, his face shaking with terror, "the room is disappearing from me still!"

"Take my hand and honestly commit your love for me, Norman, and I will stay with you always and love you forever." She reached out her hand and took his.

"Color, I see color!" he shouted. "I see red and blue and green—my precious colors have come back to me, and the room is bursting with white light, and I can see all of it! I am cured!" and he thrust away her hand, but when he did, he screamed once more, crying, "My precious colors are gone again, and the room is fading from view!"

Once again she reached out and took his hand, and once again the vibrant colors of the world revealed themselves to him and the full dimensions of the room appeared to him; but once again he thrust her hand away, and once more the colors vanished and the dimensions of the room shrank further still to his eyes. "You have bewitched me!" he shouted at her.

"It is only love, Norman, it is only love that can save you now, love will heal you, love that you have pushed away—simple, elegant, life-giving love—and you have only to reach out," she said, and she grasped his hand once more, "and declare your love for me."

Now, even though the transliteration of his profusely grotesque language will continue, it is necessary to cite where and when he placed this ugly verbiage that is generally unacceptable within the borders of modern civilization. After throwing her hand away, he proceeded to curse her and curse her family and friends, and curse the hospital and doctors; and as he did so, the room, as if these profane words could indeed take on the nature of colors, was covered in the darkest, filthiest black sludge, and dripping with the freshly spilled red blood that it had siphoned off the woman over the years; and lo, the woman rose, and as she did so, these colors that desecrated every living thing and every inanimate object quivered and pulled away from her as she walked, and everywhere she walked, the room lit up and purged the wicked colors that still spewed out of his gaping mouth.

He went blind even though the doctors never found anything organically wrong with him. He went home to an empty house and sought to live as a man with sight lives, but he failed, and hired a woman to live there and take care of his every need. He thought he could treat this woman as he had treated Jean, but this woman merely turned her back on him and quit after three days; he hired another woman and treated her as he treated all other people, but she merely turned her back on him and quit after two days. He flew into rages and vowed never to hire another "wet nurse," and even attempted to paint and then arrange to sell his drawings to local art galleries. One owner did show up, and upon viewing the gnarled, twisted images on the canvas, abruptly turned and quit the place. He was wealthy yet could spend the money on anything he could enjoy; he was an artist and could not paint;

he was a tyrant yet had no one to bully; he was arrogant yet there was no one he could bludgeon with his condescension; to wit, there was no one to freely take in his premeditated and industrious outbursts, and consequently he was suffocating on his own emotional vomit.

Months later, the police broke into the place and found the mummified body of Norman Rotweiller—he had rubbed incenses and spices all over his body and then wrapped himself in strips of cloth and then lay on his work table until he starved to death. He had left a note that said, "I leave my body—a living artwork—to science, so they might determine the origin of my genius." An art dealer from an unspecific country offered a million dollars for the corpse.

It was later rumored that a certain billionaire had a collection of stuffed bodies of celebrities in his giant cellar; in one corner there was the eerie, still figure of a five-star general in a green military uniform with a raised ivory-handled pistol in his right hand; and across from him, the figure of a notorious criminal holding a black machine gun; and next to him, there was the full figure of a female movie star wearing a sparkling white evening gown; and next to her, holding a wooden paintbrush in his hand and an easel in the other, there was the frightening figure of a painter with a contorted face and eyes that were black hollow pits.

It did not take Jean long to truly live again, and after she inherited a great fortune, she considered the rest of humanity, and then said to herself, "I have my freedom now, and all the wealth in the world cannot purchase one second of it from me; and I grieve for those who have been denied the natural gift of freedom because of who they are and where they are and what they do not have; it is not right, and it should not be, so I will right a wrong, and if I can help only one person, then it shall be like a miracle to set that person free, for they are a world unto themselves and as important as any other person, despite their geography or gender, creed or color, or station in life; and then that person will be free to help their neighbor; and I believe this is the way of the world, that we who are able should help those who are not."

And so Jean took the money that her husband had amassed and gave every penny of it to organizations around the world that had dedicated themselves to offering succor to those people who have far too little in a world where too many people have far too much.

-Finis-

Ten Chances

When he was just a child, his parents noticed that little Ike would often melt into fits of uncontrollable rage and sometimes strike his small companions for no apparent reason, and as parents often do, they attributed these episodes to his immature age or blamed the victims; and so, in the end, they marked it all down as an anomaly.

This was the first chance.

After little Ike entered elementary school, when his Teacher happened to call his mother and father, it was nearly always about the violent acts little Ike was committing against his peers. I feel awful calling so often, the contrite Teacher would explain to the parents, but I have to protect the other children from his aggressive personality. Now, the parents of little Ike did not like that—what they considered derogatory language—one little bit, and they told the Teacher so, blaming the other children for inciting poor little Ike into hitting them; and so they eventually went to the Principal and had the child removed to another kindergarten class. Two weeks later, the new Teacher called the parents to report that he had bloodied the nose of a girl by punching her full in the face. The parents, in the office of the Principal, countered that according to little Ike, the girl had attacked him and he was merely defending himself, and that they always told him to report such abuse to the Teacher; at which point, the Teacher, aghast, said, very plainly and very succinctly, that the majority of children who attack other children always have a ready excuse—and one that they know is readily accepted by their gullible parents—to explicate their infractions. Little Ike was suspended, and the parents went to the district office to register an official complaint against the Teacher and the Principal. The boy was transferred to another class. A week later he smashed a boy's face with a wooden mallet, and when the Principal was about to suspend the boy again, the parents moved the child to another school.

This was the second chance.

In first grade, little Ike punched his Teacher in the stomach, and fortunately for Ike, the Principal of his new school did not like to suspend students, for such things made her look weak and unable to cope with discipline problems, but more importantly, absent students cost the school money, and being as miserly as her administrative breed dictated, she would save money where she could, where she should, and even where she shouldn't; and so she merely counseled the child and put him back into the same class; whereupon the Teacher, from that point to the end of the school year, developed ulcers and migraines and an inordinate number of fevers. Whenever little Ike was in the room, no one could function unless he allowed it, for here was his kingdom come, where he threw rants and rages, kicked and screamed, and bit and fought anyone who attempted to restrain his unnatural order of things; now, the Teacher attempted to have the boy suspended on many occasions, but the Principal took to blaming the Teacher for the boy's behavior, and when the Teacher began to send the boy to other rooms for a timeout, the Principal heard about it and cried that the Teacher was stealing the poor child's education from him, and thus forbade her from sending the boy away; and so the Teacher and the other Innocents were trapped—trapped like trembling lambkins in a concrete cage with a growing tiger— and there was absolutely nothing they could do about it but sit back and gaze in wild wonder at the ensuing mayhem spewing forth from this little wrecking crew; and it was these facts that chopped the Teacher up into little bits and pieces and gave her over to thoughts of retirement. And she was only twenty-seven.

In second grade, little Ike began to display even more adroit skills at manipulating his environs to fit his growing iron will, and despite being transferred to two other classrooms throughout the year, he grew in wisdom and wiles in what he could do to other human beings without them retaliating. In third grade, he had three Teachers, and also in fourth grade, and by fifth grade, when he walked through the door the first day of school, he knew exactly what he was going to do and knew that no one would stop him—no one; yet, it must be said that many Teachers attempted to counsel little Ike on the error of his ways—some of them actually visited Ike in his home—but he and his parents would have none of it.

By this year, he was certainly a big fellow, weighing one hundred and ten pounds, and not a pound of excess fat on his strong, agile form. He was sent to the office twenty times by five different Teachers and three different yard duty supervisors, and he was suspended once. On April fourth, he slammed a boy's head into a concrete wall because the boy had acciden-tally stepped on his brand-spanking-new, blue suede shoes. After much intense lobbying and promises of legal action by Ike's parents, the Principal blamed the other boy. Ike smiled a smirking smile of victory.

His mature actions in elementary school will constitute what is generally regarded as the third chance.

In middle school, he entered into a world that had not the time nor the patience to put up with his adolescent outbursts, and he was often punished—and still, after threats from the parents of Ike, the Principal simply transferred the boy from class to class, where the students and Teacher would then be imprisoned by the boy's insistence that he was in charge of his own fate, that no one was in authority over him and that he could manage his own affairs in the classroom and on campus; and thus, Ike would disrupt the classrooms from beginning to end with his incessant arguing and violent acts and absolutely nonsensical rambling. Guidance counselors and Teachers attempted to help him—some of them actually visited him in his home—but he and his parents would have none of it. In the eighth grade, he brought a switchblade knife to school and threatened a Teacher with it. He was suspended for five days.

This was the fourth chance.

He entered high school as if he were entering another kingdom to conquer; however, it conquered him, and when he attempted to bring a homemade bomb to school, he was squealed on by several of his peers, and this time he was expelled, and there was nothing his whining parents could do about it. He was then sent to the continuation high school, and there he encountered some interesting friends who, he realized, were right about the same things that everyone else but him was wrong about. Thus, a gang was born, and everyone knew it; everyone who had a brain inside their hard cranium and everyone who had a pair of eyes inside their bony skull and anyone who was over the age of ten knew what the gang was all about and who was the leader of the gang and what they had done. Teachers and Guidance Counselors tried to help Ike—some of them actually visited him in his home—but he and his parents rebuked them all.

This was the fifth chance.

When there was a break-in at the continuation school, everyone knew who had done it, and when the leader of the gang, Ike, and his fellow co-conspirators were interviewed about it, Ike would smile with his big toothy grin and say he had no idea what it was all about, and then when the authorities would press him on the issue, he would get good and mad and self-righteous and go into his rage about the whole world picking on him and being persecuted since he was a child because he was different from everyone else. His parents threatened to sue the school.

This was the sixth chance.

Somehow, Ike made it through the continuation high school and actually received a high school diploma, but this certificate meant nothing to him, for it was not conducive to his plans for conquest of the curious creatures who somehow inhabited his most private world.

Ike saw the planet as his planet, and everyone else on it was taking up space that he wanted and owned things that he thought he rightfully owned and had power that he reasoned was his for the taking; now, if you were not for him, you were against him, and this meant that anyone who did not agree with his plans to abduct the third planet from the sun for his own personal fiefdom was subject to annihilation. It was at about this time that he discovered the miracle of strength training.

Thus, now when he walked down the street with his loyal posse behind him, he walked with a bold swagger that proclaimed a new prince in the city, a new boss who would alter the political and social landscape with his radical ideas, a leader who boasted of having no moral restraints in his pursuit of wealth and dominance, as if there was a world out there who had been waiting for a prophet like him to rescue them from their dreary and unsatisfying lives.

When he was twenty, he severely beat a rival gang member and the police suspected him but he was able to convince one of his loyal crew to take the rap for him; Ike convinced the boy to do this by promising him great power and financial rewards when the underaged youth would get out of his brief stay in the amusement-park-juvenile-system. The authorities knew who had really done the crime but they could not prove it, so they accepted the youth as token sacrifice instead; later, Ike had the boy killed in prison.

This was the seventh chance.

Thus, emboldened now by his ability to weave in and out of trouble from birth till this moment with absurd facileness, Ike set out to do what he wanted to do. He set up a network to sell illegal drugs in the city, he moved in on the local pimps and took over their prostitutes, he set up muggings and car thefts and small business robberies, and no matter what happened or where he was, he was always home in time for supper with his mother and father, who always asked him how his day at the auto repair shop had been, and he always smiled after kissing the both of them and then would softly say that everything was just fine, and he was always sure to give them some of his too-large paycheck for such a small job he had—but his parents never questioned him about it.

This was the eighth chance.

But criminals and their criminal activities never last long when they grow too big too fast, and do not have the power backing of a larger criminal organization, and so the authorities eventually and quite easily infiltrated Ike's little gang of horrors and gained enough evidence on him to send him to prison for five years—despite desperate pleas from his sobbing parents—where he received impassioned counseling from the counselors and impassioned visits from his parents and impassioned prayers from the chaplains, and even impassioned visits from criminals who were above and beyond him in the complicated and dirty business of crime; so, yes, he was back in school, but this time he was listening attentively and not interrupting his hardened pedagogues.

When he got out of prison, his loyal posse was gone, but he had never needed them, for he was a human magnet to which all things crooked and corrupt cling; and there were always women around him, beautiful women, too, who liked his loose money and his rugged looks and his defiant talk.

Ike imagined that now he was a virtual super-being who could not be stopped merely because he had theoretical ideas about how he might flourish in society; and so, he set about to prove that he was capable of reaching the zenith of the crime world. He set up another gang, and in the meantime, he began by robbing his neighbors, and if he happened to be caught, he simply threatened to kill the victims if they talked; and as he continued on in his diligent work, he happened upon a comely woman in a home he was robbing, and raped her; this set him off on a series of home invasions involving robbery and rape and mayhem for six months—but he was always careful to threaten the victims with the promise of death if they ever squealed on him.

But things such as this, serial crimes committed by an individual with no sense of caution or reason, do not very last long, and soon the police caught him; at the trial, he was convicted of only two robberies out of the sixty-three he had actually committed, and he was found guilty of only one rape. The prosecutors knew that many of the witnesses had been intimidated by Ike's gang, and when the rape victim who had testified against him was murdered, they could not prove who did it. Ike received five more years in jail.

This was the ninth chance.

The next time he was free from jail he was more than thirty years old, and immediately he set out to violate the rights of citizens wherever and whenever he wished. He was caught and prosecuted and let go and caught and prosecuted and sent to jail for six months and then let out and he was soon back to work hurting the local citizens and yet he always came home in time for supper and was always sure to give his parents a healthy portion of his lootings.

He was watched day and night and night and day by the local police detectives, but they were constrained by weak laws and weak juries and weak judges to put Ike away into a teeny, tiny prison cell where they might seal him up for all time, for society had ordained it that he needed every chance in the world and then some, more chances and more chances and even chances after he had committed more egregious, inhuman and nonsensical acts, and even after he had committed the most heinous acts of all—even more chances, more generous chances, a seemingly perpetual amount of chances to repent and be genuinely sad and evince a big, sloppy, sad face and cry big, salty, warm tears in front of the world courts, where he would then say that he would promise to be a good boy the next time.

Ike tried to get a job so the police would lay off him for a while, but no employer—at least the kind of employer Ike desired, even those who were willing to look past his criminal record—wanted someone who had not mastered even the basic lessons in reading, writing and arithmetic; so, Ike was forced to take a job involving manual labor and he lasted about half a workday before breaking a window of the factory he was

working in and then, after storming out, robbing a local convenience store. He bashed in the skull of the manager there
and stole the money and walked out and was caught once more
and once more was sent to jail, but this time for only two years.

He was in jail for the third time but it was no charm for him,
for he soon realized that he was not going to become a big-shot
criminal but merely stay a small-time punk who had not many
brains; yes, he realized that perhaps there was something wrong
with his mind and now he was going to figure out why. So, he
thought and thought and thought about it all night as he lay on
his iron bunk and he thought and thought and thought about it
all day as he enjoyed the privileges of weight training and the
recreation room and phone time, and he thought about all of it
as he listened to the men he considered his heroes, he listened
very carefully to their angry speech and he decided that what
they were preaching about as to why they were in this bleed-
ing wound of society was the actual truth; and so, he began to
fume about this, the same way a small child fumes at his parents as he sits in the corner for his deed done wrong; and the
more he deliberated upon his fate, the more he was convinced
he knew why he was in here and not on the outside leading a
life he reasoned society owed him—one of privilege and lei-
sure because of who he was, because he was a special person,
above and beyond the rest, a person who was always smarter
and bolder than everyone else and who had always managed
to come out on top until now. He told everyone he could tell
exactly what he was going to do when he got out, and no one
seemed to believe him. He even told his parents.

This was the tenth chance.

When he got out of prison this time, he went right to the
place where he kept certain implements he needed to be com-
petent at his illicit trade, and then went straight to his old high

school and right into the office and plucked his brown semi-automatic shotgun out from under his long, black leather coat and commenced firing at the secretary, whom he killed, and the Principal, whom he killed, and a Guidance Counselor, whom he wounded, and then he fled down the stairs and casually drove to the middle school he had attended and walked right up into the office and pulled out a black semiautomatic hand-gun and shot the secretary dead and then shot the Principal dead and then fled out the door and into his car and drove casually to his last stop.

He drove into the parking lot of his old elementary school and got out, but this time he was attracted by the noise of the children on the playground, and so he went right up to the silver wire fence there and, with a bit of nostalgia welling up in his eyes, gazed upon the children and remembered the good times he had had running around this campus; but this did not last very long, because he began to remember what these mean people here had done to him, so he quickly jumped the fence and walked into the middle of the playground and opened up his long, black leather jacket to reveal an arsenal of weapons. The children around him screamed and fled pell-mell. Ike lifted up his camouflaged semiautomatic rifle and began firing.

There had been a male Teacher who was playing with his students on the playground when big Ike had unleashed his weapons, and this man, being of a strong mind and ever-stron-ger body, had quickly discerned the proper route to take to disable the monster; and so, moving swiftly, he managed to get behind Ike and tackle him and subdue him, and with more Teachers coming, Ike was caught and bound like a man-eating tiger before he could actually hurt anyone.

At the trial, the parents put forth their impassioned defense of Ike, and the defense lawyer, with a good deal of money in his greasy hands, put forth his impassioned defense of Ike; and when Ike spoke, he, curiously, put forth the same emotional defense as his parents and his lawyer.

The World, said a weeping Ike, had always given up on him, and no one had ever cared about him, and no Teacher or Guidance Counselor or Minister had ever cared about his troubles or ever tried to help him, and that was why he had begun a life of crime; but no one believed Ike anymore, for they—the aghast judge and the aghast jury—realized that Ike should have been taken care of a long, long time ago, because he had, like too many others, indulged the flesh in its corrupt desires, had no shame for his actions, and despised authority; that he was a morally despicable creature of instinct who was destined to be caught and killed like a man-eating beast; that he was a blot, a blemish, a brute that dines with you and plots against you and feasts on sin and cherishes the destruction of any good man; and so they sentenced Ike to die like the mad dog he was in that O-so-permanent fixer of humans-turned-wild-animals, that O-so-uncomfortable, O-so-creepy-looking, custom-crafted, humble electric chair.

And so there were no more chances for Ike now, and no more chances for the people he had killed, too; and for those he had hurt, there were no more chances to live as if they had not been assaulted by a human missile of indeterminate and unlimited destruction, for society had had its chances long ago, but had been unwilling and afraid to take them. And that is the way it is in a world that hands out too many chances to too many people who have freely chosen to hunt Innocents in society for pleasure, profit and power.

-Finis-

www.ingramcontent.com/pod-product-compliance
Lightning Source LLC
Chambersburg PA
CBHW020246150626
46552CB00020B/574